Emma Wynn's Ideal Husband:

1) He must be devoted first to his wife and family—everything else comes second.

2) He can't have rugged good looks or sexy blue eyes—you'll never win an argument with a man that irresistible.

3) He shouldn't make your heart pound too loudly—otherwise you won't be able to listen to your own common sense.

4) He shouldn't be the town charmer. Just because your friends like him doesn't mean he's right for you.

5) He definitely would *not* be Michael Flint.

Dear Reader,

Ah, summertime...those lazy afternoons and sultry nights. The perfect time to find romance with a mysterious stranger in a far-off land, or right in your own backyard—with an irresistible Silhouette Romance hero. Like Nathan Murphy, this month's FABULOUS FATHER. Nathan had no interest in becoming a family man, but when Faith Reynolds's son, Cory, showed him *The Daddy List,* Nathan couldn't help losing his heart to the boy, and his pretty mom.

The thrills continue as two strong-willed men show their women how to trust in love. Elizabeth August spins a stirring tale for ALWAYS A BRIDESMAID! in *The Bridal Shower.* When Mike Flint heard that Emma Wynn was about to marry another man, he was determined to know if her love for him was truly gone, or burning deep within. In Laura Anthony's *Raleigh and the Rancher* for WRANGLERS AND LACE, ranch hand Raleigh Travers tries her best to resist ranch owner Daniel McClintock. Can Daniel's love help Raleigh forget her unhappy past?

Sometimes the sweetest passions can be found right next door, or literally on your doorstep, as in Elizabeth Sites's touching story *Stranger in Her Arms* and the fun-filled *Bachelor Blues* by favorite author Carolyn Zane.

Natalie Patrick makes her writing debut with the heartwarming *Wedding Bells and Diaper Pins.* Winning custody of her infant godson seemed a lost cause for Dani McAdams until ex-fiancé Matt Taylor offered a marriage of convenience. But unexpected feelings between them soon began to complicate their convenient arrangement!

Happy Reading!

Anne Canadeo
Senior Editor

Please address questions and book requests to:
Silhouette Reader Service
U.S.: 3010 Walden Ave., P.O. Box 1325, Buffalo, NY 14269
Canadian: P.O. Box 609, Fort Erie, Ont. L2A 5X3

Elizabeth August

The Bridal Shower

Silhouette
ROMANCE™
Published by Silhouette Books
America's Publisher of Contemporary Romance

To Sue and Bud...
Your many years of love and devotion to one another has
long been an inspiration to me.

 SILHOUETTE BOOKS

ISBN 0-373-19091-3

THE BRIDAL SHOWER

CAST OF CHARACTERS

The Women:

Hannah Farley:	Blue-blooded bad girl.
Emma Wynn:	Once burned, twice shy.
Sophie Reynolds:	Single mom with secrets.
Lucy Maguire:	Not left at the altar for long.
Katie Jones:	Always a bridesmaid…

The Men:

Matthew Granger:	Stranger in a small town.
Michael Flint:	Mr. Wrong has never been so right.
Ford Maguire:	Lucy's lawman brother falls for shady lady?
Max Ryder:	Mystery man appears in the nick of time.
Luke Cassidy:	Single dad makes impassioned plea.

Can Michael stop Emma from marrying Mr. Right Enough? Will Ford uncover Sophie's secrets?

The Always a Bridesmaid! series continues each month in a different Silhouette line. Look for the flash next month in Intimate Moments.

Books by Elizabeth August

ELIZABETH AUGUST

lives in western North Carolina, with her husband, Doug, and her three boys, Douglas, Benjamin and Matthew. She began writing romances soon after Matthew was born. She's always wanted to write.

Elizabeth does counted cross-stitching to keep from eating at night. It doesn't always work. "I love to bowl, but I'm not very good. I keep my team's handicap high. I like hiking in the Shenandoahs, as long as we start up the mountain so the return trip is down rather than vice versa." She loves to go to Cape Hatteras to watch the sun rise over the ocean.

Elizabeth August has also published books under the pseudonym Betsy Page.

Chapter One

Emma Wynn frowned impatiently as she drove up to The Clover Street Boarding House, which was owned and operated by her friend Katie Jones. Parking in front of the pale yellow three-story residence she glanced at the car clock. She was fifteen minutes late for Hannah Farley's bridal shower. She hated being late for anything. Normally she would have showed up early and helped Katie with the last-minute preparations.

Well, her tardiness wasn't her fault. It was Mike Flint's fault! Her father was up to something and she was positive it involved the blond-haired, blue-eyed charter boat captain. And, whatever *it* was, she had a feeling she wasn't going to approve. Mike Flint and her father were cut from the same cloth.

Forget about them, she ordered herself as she parked. Concentrate on Hannah. This is her day.

Quickly she made a check of her appearance in the vanity mirror behind the sun visor. Her short, wavy black hair was in place and the new gray eye shadow she was trying out for the first time did seem to accent the green of her eyes. Or maybe it was the frustration left from her unsuccessful probing into her father's planned escapade that was giving them an extra glint. Either way, I'll pass muster, she decided. She picked up the gift lying on the passenger seat and climbed out of her car.

To her relief, the sense of welcome exuded by Katie's homey-appearing, well-cared-for boarding house helped ease her tension as she mounted the steps and entered. From the front parlor she heard laughter and she felt herself relax and smile as she joined Hannah and the other guests.

Hannah seemed to actually be glowing with joy. Lucky girl, Emma thought, hoping that one day she'd be glowing like that at her own shower. And I will, she assured herself. After all she was only twenty-five. She had plenty of time to find her Mr. Right. And maybe she already had.

A few minutes later, Emma had successfully put her father and Mike Flint out of her mind and was joining in some playful teasing when she heard the front screened door bang closed.

"Oops," a woman's harried voice muttered apologetically.

Next came a baby's cry quickly followed by soothing words from the same harried female voice.

"Sounds like someone needs assistance," Emma said, the last words issued over her shoulder as she hurried out into the hall to offer aid. There, just inside the front door was a woman Emma judged to be in her late twenties. She was thin and pale with brown hair and blue eyes, holding a baby in one arm and carrying a small suitcase in her free hand.

Noticing the woman's nervousness, Emma glanced at the baby. "What a lovely child," she said in a friendly tone, hoping to put the new arrival at ease.

The woman smiled with motherly pride. "She is a dear." Then abruptly, the smile vanished as quickly as it had appeared. In a businesslike tone, she asked, "Are you the proprietress?"

"I am," Katie Jones replied, coming out of the living room at that moment.

The woman's attention immediately shifted from Emma to the brown-haired, green-eyed, pleasant-looking owner of the boarding house. "I'm Sophie Reynolds. I was wondering if you have a room to let to my daughter and me." Her businesslike demeanor faltered letting her nervousness show through. "I hope you don't mind children."

Katie smiled. "Yes, I have a room and, no, I don't mind children at all."

As Katie's gaze fell on the child, Emma was sure she saw a fleeting expression of wistfulness cross her friend's features.

"How old is your baby?"

At the sound of yet another voice, Emma glanced over her shoulder to see that Hannah and the rest of the party had joined them.

"Six months," Sophie replied.

"She's adorable," Hannah cooed.

Her gaze flickering over the growing assemblage, apology showed on Sophie's face. "I hope I'm not interrupting anything."

"Hannah's getting married and we're giving her a bridal shower," Katie explained.

An embarrassed flush darkened Sophie's cheeks. "I'm really sorry I intruded."

"The more the merrier," Hannah replied. "Katie has prepared enough food for an army. Please, come and join us after you've put your things in your room."

Sophie smiled at Hannah's kindness. "Thank you for the invitation. But I'm really rather tired."

"In that case, why don't I get you registered and up to your room," Katie suggested gently.

"I'll wait until you return before I open any gifts," Hannah promised.

"In the meantime, we'll busy ourselves eating and gossiping," Emma added. Mischief suddenly sparked in her eyes. "Just remember, anyone not present is fair game."

Katie rewarded this playful threat with her usual quiet smile. Then insisting on carrying Sophie's suitcase, she led the woman down the hall.

"I love the smell of babies," Hannah said as the rest of the group returned to the living room.

"First we have to get you married, then you can begin indulging your other cravings," one of the women quipped and a flood of fresh teasing began.

Seating herself in one of the two chintz-covered wing chairs that stood on either side of the fireplace, Emma's gaze traveled around the room. There were knickknacks on the tables and fresh cut flowers on the mantel. The furniture was comfortable and seemed to invite a person to sit and relax. This room, she thought, was one that could be found in any well-loved home. In fact, this boarding house felt more like a true residence than a business establishment, she mused.

Then recalling her jest about gossiping about anyone not present, she frowned thoughtfully. Even if she had a tendency to gossip, which she didn't, there wasn't anything she could say about Katie. Her frown suddenly deepened. Of course there had been that momentary wistfulness she was sure she'd seen on her friend's face when Katie had looked at Sophie Reynold's baby.

Almost immediately another remembered scene crossed Emma's mind. It had happened in the Beauty Boutique. Emma, Hannah and Katie had all been there getting their hair done. Jeannie Potts, one of the beauticians, had mentioned to Katie that she'd heard Luke Cassidy had a child. Katie had seemed to freeze for a brief moment. Then she'd made some noncommittal response and quickly turned the conversation to brands of shampoos.

Hannah, too, had obviously noticed Katie's momentary lapse because very quietly, when Katie wouldn't notice, Hannah had reminded Emma that Katie and Luke Cassidy had once been an item. Emma had mentally kicked herself for forgetting. But then that had been a long time ago and, after the man had left town, Katie had never mentioned his name again.

"You look like a woman with something on your mind." Hannah's voice broke into Emma's thoughts.

"Just a momentary flight of fancy," Emma hedged, respecting Katie's privacy too much to say what she'd been thinking.

"I don't suppose it would have anything to do with Mike Flint?" Susan Marley asked, curiosity strong in her eyes. "I saw him coming out of your house yesterday."

"It definitely did not have anything to do with Mike Flint," Emma assured her.

"If that tall, rugged sailor came knocking on my door, I'd be giving him a few moments of thought," Susan mused wistfully.

Emma started to wish Susan all the luck in the world with Mike Flint but the words refused to issue. I wouldn't wish being married to a man whose heart already belongs to the sea on anyone, she reasoned to account for her hesitation. "He only stopped by to see my father," she said instead, wanting to be certain everyone in the room understood that there was nothing going on between her and Mike.

"I think Emma is more interested in having Kenneth Drake on her doorstep," Hannah interjected, a knowing gleam in her eyes.

Susan grinned at Emma. "I did hear you and Kenneth were seeing each other. How serious is it? Should we be expecting to attend another bridal shower soon?"

"I never make predictions," Emma hedged. Uncomfortable being the center of attention, she added, "I thought this was Hannah's day. We should be concentrating on her."

"Here comes Katie," Judy Lewes announced from near the doorway.

"Gift opening time," several voices chorused in unison.

Emma breathed a sigh of relief to have the attention of everyone turned elsewhere. It had been almost four months now since she'd first met Kenneth Drake and begun dating him. He was the golf pro at a local country club; a solid, dependable man with both feet planted firmly on land. She and Kenneth both had the same likes and dislikes and had, right away, found each other comfortable companions. She felt there was a strong possibility that he would ask her to marry him. But she found herself hesitant about admitting this to anyone. He's exactly the husband I've been waiting for, she admonished herself, hating the sudden uneasiness that swept through her.

In the next instant she was assuring herself that she wasn't nervous about marrying Kenneth. It was the thought of marriage in general that unnerved her, she affirmed. After all, it was a very big commitment. Shoving Kenneth out of her mind, she joined in the fun of watching Hannah opening her gifts.

By the time the shower ended, Emma was feeling relaxed and happy as she gave Hannah a hug, wished her well, then left. But when she climbed in behind the wheel of her car, her smile began to fade. Her father had spent every evening this week studying nautical charts. He'd owned his own charter boat for more than twenty-five years and fished the Atlantic off the coast of Clover, South Carolina, all his life. Experience plus a certain amount of innate instinct told him where the fish would be. He didn't need any charts for that.

And then last night when she arrived home from work, she'd seen Mike Flint leaving as she pulled up. Like her father, Mike owned his own boat and chartered it out to tourists. He also owned a salvaging rig. The suspicion that had been nagging her before she'd arrived at the bridal shower returned.

At the corner, she signaled for a turn that would take her home but then paused and glanced at her watch. It was nearly eleven on a Monday night. A little late to be calling on anyone, she admitted. On the other hand, if she was going to catch Mike Flint at home, this would be a better time than most.

"I could drive by his place and if the lights are on, I'll stop," she decided aloud, using the sound of her own voice to bolster her resolve. A few minutes later, as she drove past the two-story house on the quiet tree-lined street, she noted that several lights were still burning. A blue pickup truck was parked in the driveway. She knew it belonged to Mike. Not wanting to interrupt his evening if he had company, she quickly scanned for any other vehicle that would indicate he might not be alone. There were none.

Parking in front of his house, she got out and walked with a purposeful stride toward the front door. Halfway there, the sudden thought that his neighbors might see her caused a hesitation in her step. Too late to worry about that now, she chided herself and continued.

Her gaze took in the weeded gardens and the fresh paint job, completed just this past summer on the entire house, and she was forced to admit that Mike Flint kept his home in as good a repair as he kept his boats.

Reaching his door, she rapped twice sharply with the cast-iron knocker.

From inside she heard footsteps approaching, then the door opened. Emma stood five feet five inches tall in her stocking feet. But even with the added height of the three-inch high heels she was wearing, his six foot one inch frame seemed to tower over her. It was his physique, she realized, that made him seem so large. Years of hard labor had given him the muscular build of an athlete. His blond hair, bleached even blonder by the sun, was a bit shaggy around the ears and long enough that it curled slightly at his nape. Eyes as blue as the ocean studied her coolly. He looks like the sea-roving rogue he is, she thought.

"Emma Wynn. This is a surprise," he said, breaking the silence between them. Suddenly concern showed on his face. "Has something happened to your father?"

"Nothing yet," she replied curtly, her tone implying that should anything happen to Peter Wynn, she might very easily be the cause.

"Maybe you should come in," he suggested, stepping aside to allow her to enter.

She found herself hesitating. Being alone with Mike Flint had always made her nervous. Mentally fussing at herself for letting his presence intimidate her, she accepted his invitation, continuing just far enough into the foyer to give him room to close the door and leave some distance between them. As the latch clicked, ensuring their conversation would be private, she leveled her gaze on him. "I want to know what you and my father are up to."

He regarded her thoughtfully. "Shouldn't you be asking him?"

She scowled impatiently. "I have but he's got a talent for being evasive when he wants to be."

"Maybe if you asked him as one adult to another instead of sounding as if you consider both him and me something akin to two kids planning a prank, he might be more talkative," he suggested dryly.

The impatience on her face increased. "I did." Emma's nerves were near the breaking point. "Look, I don't like having to come here," she snapped, then flushed when she realized how blunt she'd been.

"I didn't invite you," he reminded her tersely, anger beginning to grow in his eyes.

A confrontation was not going to help her find out the truth, she cautioned herself. "I apologize. I didn't mean that the way it sounded. It's embarrassing to me to have to go behind my father's back to find out what he's up to. But he's all I have left in the world and I don't want anything to happen to him."

"I consider your father a friend. You have my word, I'll do everything in my power to see that no harm comes to him."

Emma was more certain by the moment that she knew what her father was up to. "He wants to go looking for the wreckage of that yacht that went down in the spring, the one the owner has offered two hundred thousand dollars for the retrieval of the safe that was on board, doesn't he?" she demanded.

"He has a few ideas about where it might be." Mike conceded.

Emma's stomach knotted. "Larry Kiefer had a few ideas and nearly got himself killed."

"Kiefer takes unnecessary risks. I don't."

"Salvaging in the ocean is always a risk," she declared curtly. "Even on the inland waterways, it can be dangerous. I've done some diving. I know about shifting currents and unfriendly predators."

"Walking across the street can get you killed," he rebutted. "Look, you have my word. I'll keep an eye on your father."

Emma had never doubted that Mike Flint could take care of himself but suddenly she found herself feeling apprehensive for him as well. "I wouldn't want to see you getting hurt, either."

He grinned cynically as if he didn't totally believe her. "It's nice to know you care."

Considering the fact that, normally, she would cross the street to avoid encountering him and he knew it, she couldn't blame him for his sarcasm. "To put it more accurately, I don't want you on my conscience. And if you were to get hurt because of some foolish notion of my father's, I'd feel responsible."

"I've taken care of myself for a long time. And I accept the sole responsibility for my actions."

Emma had never felt so frustrated. "You're determined to aid and abet my father, aren't you?"

He scowled at the accusation in her voice. "Your father is a grown man, not a child. And he is determined to pursue this. I'm going along to keep an eye on him. I owe him. He was a good friend to my grandfather and has been one to me."

Emma glared at him. "Men!" She lowered her voice, and giving a good imitation of a "salty sailor" said in mimicking tones, "He's me buddy and a mate.

If he decides to walk into the fires of hell, I'll foller with a sprinkling can.''

A hint of a smile played at the corner of Mike's mouth. Then it was gone and his scowl was back. ''You're exaggerating.''

Deciding to take another ploy, she asked sharply, ''What about his and your charter businesses and your more practical salvage operations? Surely you can't afford to just walk away from them and spend your time on a wild-goose chase?''

A patronizing expression came over his face. ''Neither of us is going to walk away from our businesses. We'll look for the safe in our spare time.''

''Anything to keep you on the water and away from your home on the land,'' she muttered.

Mike's gaze narrowed on her as if he was seeing something he'd missed before. ''Look, if you want to spend more time with your father, I'm sure he'd enjoy having you crew with him on the weekends like you used to do when you were a kid.''

Emma frowned to cover her embarrassment. She couldn't believe that remark had slipped out. She'd determined ages ago that the feeling of being neglected by her father was childish. And she was beyond childish emotions. ''I don't consider baiting hooks and looking after seasick tourists a real enjoyable way to spend my spare time.''

''I suppose lolling around the country club with Drake is your idea of fun and excitement,'' he taunted.

''As a matter of fact it is,'' she assured him tartly.

His expression hardened. ''Then I suggest you go have your fun and leave me and your father to have ours.''

"Men!" she seethed again. Then admitting that she was doing no good here, she flung open the door and stalked out.

Driving home, she wanted to issue a primordial scream. "I read once where that was supposed to relieve stress," she mused under her breath, attempting to work up her courage to try it. But her conservative nature held her back. With the luck she'd been having today, someone would probably report her for disturbing the peace and she was in no mood to explain her actions to Sheriff Maguire.

Arriving home, she paused to stare up at the starlit sky before going inside. Her mother had been dead now for nearly nine years. Still at moments like this, Emma felt as if Nancy Wynn was somehow present. "Mom, how in the world did you find the patience to put up with Dad?" she spoke quietly to the sky above. Her jaw firmed. "I love him dearly, but I will never marry a man whose heart belongs to the sea."

Chapter Two

Emma groaned. She'd set her alarm for five so she could be up in time to have a talk with her father before he left for the marina. Dropping her head back onto her pillow, she considered waiting until the evening. But he could get a night charter and then she might not see him until tomorrow evening.

Climbing out of bed, she headed to the bathroom. A few minutes later, still in her nightgown and terry-cloth robe, but with her teeth brushed and her face washed so that she was more awake, she headed to the kitchen.

"Morning, girl," her father greeted her, surprise at seeing her at this early hour evident on his face. Worry replaced the surprise. "You're not sick, are you?"

"No," she replied, continuing to the counter and pouring herself a cup of coffee. Peter Wynn was a stoutly built man, standing a little under six feet tall.

But Emma knew that very little of his bulk, if any, was flab. Now fifty, his once dark brown hair was showing marked signs of graying and his face, still handsomely featured, was deeply lined and had an almost leathery appearance from a lifetime of being on the water in the sun. Turning back, she saw him grinning at her affectionately.

"You look more and more like your mother every day," he said. "That same raven black hair and those sea green eyes. 'Course your mother used to wear her hair long. Now that ain't saying I don't like your style. But I remember the first time I saw her standing on the beach, the wind blowing through those black tresses. Prettiest woman I'd ever seen or ever have seen, excepting you."

Emma couldn't stop herself from grinning. "You could charm the whiskers off a catfish." She knew she had a pleasant enough face but she wasn't a raving beauty. Still, he made her feel as if she was. Don't let him deter you, she warned herself. Her expression hardened. "I stopped by to see Mike Flint last night. And he confirmed a suspicion I've had for the past week. You're thinking of searching for that sunken yacht. You could get yourself as well as Mike killed. And what about your business? You can't afford to neglect that."

He held up his hand like a traffic cop stopping an oncoming car. "Now, don't go getting your shackles up. We're only going hunting for the yacht when we have the time. And we'll be careful."

Emma continued to frown. "I don't like it."

"The weather hasn't been good to us," her father reminded her. "Business has been slow. That salvage money would come in handy. Besides, we'd be doing a real service. That Meldon fellow who owned the yacht only wants the safe back because it contains his private diary and photographs of his kids and late wife. We're talking about a man's memories. In the end, they can be life's most precious treasures."

Emma saw the shadow of sadness cross her father's features and knew he was again thinking of her mother. "I suppose," she conceded. "But I still don't like it."

The shadow passed and a gleam returned to Peter Wynn's eyes. "Finding that yacht is also a matter of pride. For the past four months every young know-it-all who thinks he knows this ocean has been out searching with their fancy equipment. Even Mike took one swing out to look for it. But not one of them found a trace. Me, all I've got is this..." He pointed to his nose.

"That proboscis of yours has sometimes led you down the path to trouble," Emma reminded him.

"I'll admit, I've sometimes thought I was sniffing a rose and it turned out to be an onion," he agreed, then grinned broadly. "But onions give the flavor to the stew." As he made this declaration, he rose from the table and approached her. Before she could respond, he placed a light kiss on her nose and said, "I've enjoyed our little father-daughter chat, but I've got to run. I've got a charter who wants to cast off at the crack of dawn."

Unable to allow him to leave without wishing him well, she called out to his departing back, "Have a safe day." But as the door swung closed behind him, frustration filled her. "Onions," she growled under her breath, and shook her head.

As if it were yesterday she saw herself and her mother standing in this kitchen. She was twelve and tears of disappointment were streaming down her cheeks. They'd just returned from the school play in which she'd had a part. Even though it was a small part, she'd been so proud and she'd wanted desperately for her father to be there to see her perform. But he'd gotten busy making a repair on his boat and forgotten about the time.

"Your father is not going to change to suit you," her mother was saying. "He loves us, but he loves the sea and his boat just as much. You're simply going to have to learn to accept him the way he is."

The image faded and Emma breathed a resigned sigh. The play hadn't been the first time he'd missed an important moment in her life nor was it the last. But he had been repentant each time and she had one of the largest assortments of dolls in town as proof he was truly sorry. And the collection continued to grow. To this day, when he thought he'd gotten on her bad side, he'd show up with a prettily wrapped box that contained another doll. Shaking her head at herself for losing two hours of sleep on what she should have known all along would be a futile effort, she took a sip of her coffee, then set it aside and went upstairs to dress.

Emma straightened from unloading a box of books, stretched, then glanced at her watch. It was nearly noon. The morning seemed to have flown past. Her gaze traveled around the stockroom of Balanski's

Bookstore. She'd managed to unpack, inventory and shelve more than half of the shipment that had arrived yesterday afternoon.

Deciding she deserved a break, she poured herself a cup of coffee and sank into one of the two comfortable upholstered chairs on either side of the small table in front of the window that faced the property behind the building. The view beyond was of a lovingly tended garden. She was well aware that not all bookstores had such pleasant amenities as this one. But Balanski's was a privately owned business and run with what Martha Balanski liked to term a congenial, refined air.

The store was housed in an elegant old residence just off Clover Street. The downstairs had been renovated to create a comfortable browsing atmosphere for the customers. The upper floor housed an office and an apartment where Martha Balanski lived.

Emma smiled with satisfaction as she surveyed all she'd accomplished. At least the energy generated by her anxiousness over her father's latest escapade had been put to good use.

"You look tired."

Surprised by the edge of accusation in the familiar male voice, Emma turned to the door of the stockroom to see Kenneth Drake standing there. Even angry, the thirty-one-year-old golf pro would be considered handsome by anyone's standards, she thought. The anger only seemed to accent the classic lines of his face. And standing six foot two with an athletic build gave him an impressive presence. Then there was his thick, light brown hair cut conservatively on the sides and top but left to hang collar length in the back. And, as Katie had once remarked, he did have the softest doe brown eyes. However, at the moment, they were more of a hickory color and definitely held no softness, Emma noted, realizing she'd never seen him this angry with her before. "I am a little," she admitted. "I've been unpacking books and restocking shelves all morning."

"Maybe if you got to bed earlier at night, you'd have more energy for your work," he suggested caustically, entering the room and closing the door, clearly wanting to ensure their privacy.

A sudden suspicion as to what was causing his hostility toward her occurred to Emma. "You heard that I was at Mike Flint's place last night, didn't you?" she asked bluntly.

The scowl on his face deepened. "From three different sources. First there was Mayabelle Appleton. She decided she just had to come in for a lesson in getting rid of her slice...something she is never going to do because she won't keep her head still. And while I was explaining, for the thousandth time, about the necessity of keeping her head in the correct position, she suddenly mentions that she saw your car outside of Mike Flint's house around midnight. Then she abruptly declares that she needs a cup of tea more than a lesson and saunters off."

Emma mentally kicked herself. She'd forgotten that Mrs. Appleton, perhaps the premier busybody in Clover, lived only a couple of houses down and across the street from Mike.

"Mrs. Appleton was followed by Evelyn Martin, who informed me she thinks of me as a son..." He paused and, in spite of his anger, a grin tilted one corner of his mouth. "Well, actually a nephew. She corrected herself, when it occurred to her how old she'd have to admit to being if she claimed to be old enough to be my mother."

Emma grinned back hoping to encourage his sense of humor to overcome his ire at her. It didn't work.

His frown returned. "Either way," he continued tersely, "she went on to say she doesn't want to see me made a fool of when she has a lovely, marriageable daughter who would never treat a man badly."

Emma was tempted to mention that Mrs. Martin's daughter, who had just turned twenty-nine her last birthday, had already been married and divorced twice. However, reading the continued anger in Kenneth's eyes, she decided that this was not the time to point this out.

"And finally there was Henry Gleeson. He informed me that he'd outlived three wives and advised me to find a plain, uneducated woman whose only hobbies were cooking and housekeeping. Then I was to keep her pregnant and at home all of the time."

"I knew his last wife and she wasn't the least bit like that. And, from what I've heard, neither of his other two were, either," Emma pointed out. "They were all beauties who loved to party all night."

"He said he wanted me to learn from his mistakes," Kenneth returned. His gaze leveled on her. "Before I go back to the club to face my afternoon sessions, I want to know what's going on. I thought you were supposed to be attending Hannah's bridal shower last night."

"I did, but afterward I stopped by Mike Flint's place," Emma admitted.

"You just stopped by Mike Flint's place," he repeated sarcastically. "I realize you and I have never made a formal commitment but I thought we had an understanding. I thought we weren't seeing other people. In fact, the general population in this town has us labeled as a pair."

In spite of the fact that she didn't like having him angry with her, she'd been feeling flattered that he was jealous. Now she found herself wondering if he was jealous or simply embarrassed. "I'm not seeing Mike Flint. I went by to talk to him about my father," she replied.

The scowl remained on his face. "At midnight?"

"It wasn't midnight. It more like eleven," she corrected, knowing this was a weak defense but feeling the need to say it anyway. Letting her anxiety show, she continued, "I was worried about my father. I knew he was planning another of his escapades and I knew Mike was involved. I wanted to nip it in the bud."

"And did you?" he asked dryly, clearly already guessing the answer.

"No," she admitted.

He shook his head as if to say she should have known her efforts would be futile. Then his sympathy won out and his anger began to fade. "You should know by now that you can't change your father."

"You're right." Apology showed on her face. "I'm sorry if I caused you any embarrassment this morning."

His anger now gone, he shrugged. "I should have known it was something like that." Approaching her, he kissed her lightly. "You're a woman I can trust, Emma. I appreciate that."

She breathed a mental sigh of relief. "And I appreciate you being so understanding. Going by Mike Flint's place last night was foolish."

"Consider it forgotten," he replied. He placed another light kiss on her lips. "I'll be by to pick you up at six. We're having cocktails at the Evanses' before going to dinner at the club tonight."

"Six," she repeated.

He gave her a final smile, then left.

"I have got to be more discreet," she admonished herself as she got out her lunch and reseated herself by the window. Luckily for her, Kenneth was such an understanding man . . . perfect husband material, she added.

"Looks like you and Kenneth patched up your differences." Martha Balanski's voice broke into Emma's thoughts.

Looking to the door, she saw the tall, willow-thin, white-haired, seventy-year-old proprietress entering.

"I suppose it had something to do with your midnight call on Mike Flint," Martha concluded, curiosity sparkling in her eyes.

Emma gave an exaggerated groan. "Does the whole world know about that?"

"What Mayabelle Appleton knows does not remain a secret."

Emma grimaced. "Doesn't that woman ever sleep?"

"Apparently not at midnight," Martha replied with a mischievous grin.

"It wasn't midnight, it was eleven." Emma again defended herself. "And it was hardly a social call. I went by to talk to Mike about some business he has with my father."

Martha nodded knowingly. "So your father has decided to go looking for that safe and he's roped Mike into helping him."

Emma stared at the woman. "How'd you guess?"

"Nearly every local with an oceangoing vessel has given finding that yacht a try. I figured it was only a matter of time before your father got into the game. And I figured he'd be smart enough not to try it alone."

"He is a wily sea dog," Emma admitted, remembering the many times her mother had used that description. This usually came after her father had managed to charm his way out of some trouble he'd gotten into.

Martha continued to regard her thoughtfully. "Don't worry about your father. Seems to me he always manages to bring his ship back to shore."

"You're right," Emma agreed, deciding she might as well accept the inevitable. Her father was going to do exactly what he wanted to do. Her mother had been the only person who'd ever had any influence over him and even that had been very little when his mind was set on a particular course.

"And I know Mike Flint's a little rough around the edges but he's as levelheaded and dependable as any man I've ever known," Martha added.

In all honesty, Emma had to concede that she could not refute Martha's evaluation of Mike Flint, either.

At that moment, the bell attached to the front door rang announcing the arrival of a customer. Deciding it was time she did something herself to put a stop to whatever speculation was flying around town, Emma rose. "You sit and have a cup of coffee. I'll take care of whoever is here."

"A cup of coffee does sound good," Martha replied, without any argument.

Her shoulders squared for battle, Emma strode down the hall and into the front room. But the customer who had just entered wasn't one of the locals. In fact, Emma was fairly certain she'd never seen her before. She was a slender redhead about Emma's height and maybe a couple of years older. She had a somewhat ordinary face but there was a sense of purpose about her that would have caused her to stand out in any crowd, Emma thought. Her haircut was stylish and her makeup impeccably applied. Her clothing—a pastel green blouse and matching slacks made of fine quality silk and her designer handbag and matching shoes—marked her as one of the wealthy tourists who flocked to Clover during the summer months.

Watching Emma approach, the redhead smiled. "I'm thinking of opening a dress shop in town," she said when Emma drew nearer. "And everyone has told me how wonderfully this old home has been renovated. I hope you don't mind if I just look around to get a few ideas."

"No, of course not," Emma replied politely, noticing that the smile on the redhead's face did not reach her eyes. Instead the stranger's gaze swept over Emma. Then turning abruptly away, the newcomer gave the main room her full attention.

In spite of the swiftness of the woman's scrutiny, there had been an intensity about it that had left Emma slightly unnerved. Still, her natural politeness forced her to attempt to be helpful. "There are two other rooms off the hall."

The woman's gaze swung back to her. "Thank you, I believe I've seen enough," she said and strode out.

Through the oval window on the front door, Emma watched the redhead climb into a silver gray Porsche and drive away.

"Who was here?" Martha asked coming down the hall.

"Someone who is considering opening a dress shop in town," Emma replied, glancing down at herself. The cold calculation she'd read in the redhead's eyes when the woman had looked her over caused her to half expect to find a dirty smear across the front of her dress. There was none.

She was probably just sizing me up as a future customer and deciding that I couldn't afford her merchandise, Emma decided. Aloud, she said, "From her clothes and the car she drives, I'd say she's planning on a wealthy clientele...the country club set and some of our more affluent summer people."

Martha gave an approving nod. "The more merchants bringing customers to our town, the better, I always say."

Emma couldn't quite shake the uncomfortable sensation left by the woman's cold scrutiny. "I think I'll go finish my lunch," she said. As she walked back to the stockroom, even knowing it might be good for business, she hoped the redhead didn't open her shop next door.

Chapter Three

Emma had showered and was drying her hair in preparation for her date with Kenneth when she heard the front door open followed by the sounds of her father singing a limerick that would make a marine blush.

Her body stiffened. He only sang that when he was blurry-eyed drunk. And he only got blurry-eyed drunk when he was upset or depressed. Fighting down a rush of panic as a list of catastrophes raced through her head, she made sure her robe was securely belted, then hurried to the stairs. At the top of the flight, she came to an abrupt halt. Her father wasn't alone in the entrance hall. He was being supported by Mike Flint.

"Your dad asked Casey to call me. I guess he didn't want you coming down to the tavern to get him and he knew he couldn't make it home on his own," Mike explained, seeing her.

He was using his body as a crutch, holding her father in an upright position. Glancing at her father's legs, she knew they would collapse without Mike's support. "Thanks," she said stiffly, embarrassed to have anyone, even Mike Flint see her father like this.

Mike shrugged. "He'd have done the same for me."

And probably has, Emma added to herself, then turned her full attention to her father. "What happened? I thought you had a charter today."

"A newlywed couple," he said, bobbing his head up and down in an exaggerated nod. Tears suddenly welled in his eyes. "They were so much in love. Reminded me of your mother and me."

Emma felt hot tears forming behind her own eyes. Her father had his faults but he'd loved her mother as strongly as any man could love a woman. She knew without a doubt that if he could have willed her mother's cancer into his own body and died in Nancy Wynn's place he would have done it without a second of hesitation.

"I miss her," he said gruffly.

Emma continued down the stairs to the men. "I'd better get you into bed," she said, starting to slip under his free arm and relieve Mike of his burden.

Mike hoisted her father more firmly onto his own shoulder. "I'll do it. Wouldn't want to see you fall and break that pretty neck of yours as well as your father's."

Emma started to point out that she'd been taking care of her father on her own since she was sixteen years of age, but the words stuck in her throat. She'd assumed Mike's reference to her "pretty neck" had been merely a patronizing acknowledgment of her femininity. But in the dark depths of his eyes she saw a flicker of masculine appreciation that sent a curl of heat twisting through her.

Unnerved by this reaction and realizing from the set of his jaw that arguing would be futile, she stepped back and said coolly, "If you insist." As the two men started up the stairs with her following, she admonished her body for its response to Mike Flint's rakish glance. He was not what she was looking for. She'd found what she wanted in Kenneth Drake!

Following her father's mumbled instructions, Mike had gotten him to his room by the time Emma finished having her little talk with herself. "I'll get him into bed," she said.

"I hate being a burden to you, girl." Embarrassment caused her father's already ruddy complexion to redden even more. "Mike will help me get my boots off." He made a shooing motion toward Emma. "You run along."

"I'm sure Mike has better things to do with his time," she returned, hating accepting any more help from the blond-haired sea captain.

"I don't mind," Mike spoke up, obviously sensing Peter Wynn's desire to escape the added humiliation of having his daughter put him to bed.

Emma scowled. *Men,* she fumed silently. When they were sick, they wanted you to wait on them hand and foot. At other times, they acted like an offer of aid was an invasion of their privacy. Watching Mike ease her father onto the bed, she was about to insist he go home when he turned to her.

"You look as if you were getting ready to go somewhere. Maybe you should finish getting dressed," he said with icy dismissal.

The order in his voice raised her ire. This was her home. He had no right to be bossing her around. Then again she caught a glimmer in his eyes that sent a rush of heat sweeping through her.

Until this moment, her full concern had been on her father. Now, suddenly she was acutely aware of her state of undress. The blue of Mike's eyes deepened and she had the feeling he was seeing beyond the fabric of her robe to the nakedness beneath. She expected to be angry at this mental invasion of her privacy. Instead the heat that had swept through her intensified.

Abruptly his expression turned cold and he scowled as if angry with himself.

Obviously he didn't want to be attracted to her any more than she wanted to be attracted to him, she realized. Good! she told herself. The desire to escape his company became overwhelming. "You're right. I was getting ready to go out. If you want to put my father to bed, that's fine with me."

But back in her own room, Emma hesitated as she started to take a light summer frock off its hanger. "I really should stay home in case Dad gets sick and needs help," she reasoned, then frowned at her image in the mirror. "You're just looking for an excuse to skip the Evanses' cocktail party," she accused.

Grudgingly she admitted this was true. She knew hobnobbing with the elite was important to Kenneth's career and the people who invited him into their homes did seem to honestly like him. And why shouldn't they? she asked herself. He was handsome and charming.

But as for herself, although they were always polite to her, she felt as if they were merely tolerating her presence because she was Kenneth's date. She wasn't really one of their crowd. "If Kenneth and I were married then I'd feel differently...more accepted," she assured herself. But for tonight, she wanted an escape and her father had provided her with one.

After hanging the summer dress back in her closet, she pulled on a pair of shorts, a cotton top and sneakers. She'd just finished drying and brushing her hair when Mike's voice sounded from the foot of the stairs.

"Drake's here," he called up in an emotionless tone.

From her father's room, came a loud moan. "Could you keep from bellowing, there's a man with a headache up here," he yelled back, his slurred voice clearly exposing his drunkenness.

Emma hurried to the top of the stairs to find Kenneth standing in the hall frowning at Mike with an expression that made it clear he found the man's presence there unacceptable. Hearing her approaching, he turned and his frown deepened.

"My father's under the weather," she said apologetically as she joined the men. "I really think I should stay here and take care of him."

Kenneth's gaze shifted from her to Mike and she saw the skepticism in his eyes. "My father had Casey call Mike. It's my guess he thought he could get into the house and into bed without my knowing he'd been on a binge. But I was here when they arrived."

Kenneth turned to Mike, accusation on his face. "I suppose you're an innocent bystander and Peter going on a drinking binge had nothing whatsoever to do with whatever scheme you've cooked up with him backfiring on the two of you?"

Anger etched itself into Mike's features. "I don't cook up schemes."

"My father got to thinking about my mother," Emma spoke up quickly, then was startled by how speedily she'd come to Mike's defense. Well, she was only being fair, she told herself. Aloud, she added, "Sometimes that makes him melancholy and he drinks a little too much."

Understanding spread over Kenneth's face. "Sorry," he apologized to Mike.

Mike accepted the apology with a nod. Then he turned to Emma. "I'll stay with your dad. I owe you one night's baby-sitting."

An old memory flashed through Emma's mind. She pushed it back into the shadows from which it had come. "I appreciate the offer but I really think I should stay."

"I wouldn't want you to miss a good party," he persisted.

Kenneth glanced at his watch. "I can call the Evanses and cancel."

His offer pleased her but made her feel guilty at the same time. She did not want to interfere with the furthering of his career. "That's ridiculous," she replied firmly. "Jason Evan is president of the country club and he's expecting you. Really, both of you can just run along."

Mike gave an if-that's-the-way-you-want-it shrug. "My grandfather used to say that once a woman's mind was made up, neither hell nor high water was going to change it." With a farewell nod to each of them, he added, "So I'll just be on my way," and left.

Emma saw Kenneth again glancing at his watch. "You'd better run along, too, or you'll be late," she cautioned.

He frowned indecisively. "I hate leaving you to spend the evening alone."

"I really don't mind. This will give me a chance to catch up on my reading," she said with an encouraging smile.

Still looking guilty, he kissed her, then left.

Emma expected to feel mildly deserted. Instead she found herself looking forward to a quiet evening at home. Going back upstairs, she checked on her father. He was sleeping soundly.

A few minutes later down in the kitchen, as she made herself a sandwich, she recalled a Saturday morning when she was around nine or ten years of age. She, her mother and her father were all in this very room. While her father continued to make suggestions about what to take along, she and her mother were packing a picnic lunch. They were going to spend the day on his boat, the *Nancy Belle,* named after her mother. Her mother was laughingly accusing her father of wanting to take along all the food in the refrigerator. Coming up behind her mother, he'd put his arms around her and kissed her on the neck. Her mother had seemed to actually glow with joy and there had been a loving warmth in her father's eyes Emma would never forget.

"I want to love like that and be loved like that," she admitted quietly. And she and Kenneth were growing closer with each passing day. Someday they would feel that way about each other, she assured herself.

Deciding it was too beautiful an evening to stay indoors, she carried her sandwich and a glass of iced tea out onto the front porch and curled up in the porch swing. A warm breeze carrying the scent of the ocean gently ruffled her hair. As she began to eat, Mike Flint's image returned uninvited. She recalled his reference to the unpaid debt between them. The memory she'd pushed into the shadowy recesses of her mind again came to the forefront.

The night he'd referred to had occurred six years ago when she was nineteen and Mike was twenty-four. It had been January... a particularly cold, gloomy January. Mike's paternal grandfather had been ill with the flu. Norman Flint was a crusty old sailor. Her father had sworn he was too obstinate to die but the flu had turned to pneumonia and the doctors had been unable to save him.

Emma had attended the funeral with her father. Afterward, they'd gone to the home Mike had shared with his grandfather and which now belonged to Mike. Other neighbors and friends came, too, all bearing food and drink, intending to stay and help Mike through this period of mourning. But after only a short while, he'd sent them all home saying he wanted to be alone.

Respecting his need for solitude, everyone had left. But all the way home Emma had not been able to forget the pain she'd seen in his eyes. He'd lost both of his parents in a car crash when he'd been in his early teens. He'd had no brothers or sisters. His mother's parents lived in California and, to Emma's knowledge, they'd never made any real effort to spend much time with him. She thought he also had a couple of aunts and uncles on his mother's side but, like his maternal grandparents, he rarely saw them as well.

His father had been an only child. Even though his paternal grandmother was deceased, it had been old Norman who had taken the boy in when he'd been orphaned and raised him. Emma noted that no one from the other side of the family had even made the effort to attend Norman Flint's funeral.

Thus, for all practical purposes, his grandfather was the only close family Mike had. Even more, Emma had seen the old man and his grandson together enough to know that the bond they shared had been especially strong. Now Mike had no one to share that kind of closeness with.

She remembered the terrible feeling of loss and loneliness that had enveloped her when her mother died. And she'd still had her father. The thought of Mike left totally alone to face this sad night tormented her.

By the time she and her father had reached their house, her mind had been made up. "I'm going back," she'd announced.

"He wants to be alone," her father argued.

"Ah, the insular man of the sea who must suffer his losses in solitude because 'tis the way of the lonely sailor," she'd returned, mimicking the throaty growl of an ancient mariner.

"Something like that," he'd replied matter-of-factly, ignoring the mockery in her voice.

She'd scowled at him as the image of him sitting in his chair and her sitting on the floor next to it holding his hand through the long night after her mother's funeral played through her mind. He'd barely acknowledged her presence but she'd known he needed her to be there. "Well, I don't buy it," she'd said, and without any further argument, she'd turned right around and driven back to Mike's place.

He hadn't been there. Certain she knew where to find him, she went to the marina. She reached his boat, the *Reliable Lady*, just as he was untying the lines. "Permission to come abroad," she requested.

He frowned impatiently. "I'm on my way out," he replied with dismissal.

Ignoring the law that one never boarded a boat without the captain's permission, she leapt on board.

"You could get your good clothes ruined," he growled. "Go home."

He'd made her feel like a childish nuisance, still her back had straightened with resolve. "You shouldn't be alone right now and you've sent all your friends home so you're stuck with me," she'd returned and plopped herself down in one of the fishing chairs.

For a moment he'd looked as if he was going to argue, then with a shrug, he turned away and continued casting off.

The ocean was choppy and the wind was cold. Emma knew this was not a good time to be out on the water. As they headed away from land, the wind grew stronger and its chill sharper. Emma slipped off the chair and found a more sheltered seat. Still the cold breeze found her, whipping around her, seeming to cut through the heavy fabric of her coat.

Leaving the sheltered harbor, Mike headed straight out toward the center of the horizon. The *Reliable*

Lady was large enough to sleep six comfortably but the waves tossed it around as if it were a rowboat. Emma braced herself and snuggled into an even tighter ball. Looking up at the bridge, she saw him standing like a statue, his back and shoulders rigid as if challenging the ocean to a duel. A wave so strong she was sure they were going to capsize hit them but Mike never flinched.

"Playing Russian roulette with the sea is a loser's game," she muttered under her breath. Fighting the wind and the jostling motion of the boat, she climbed up onto the bridge. There she could see the grim set of his jaw and the grief etched into his features. She laid a hand on his arm to get his attention. "It's time to put back into port," she said with firm command.

Even through the fabric of his coat she was aware of the muscle beneath her palm tightening as if startled by the contact. She thought she'd never touched an arm that felt so strong.

Before he could respond, another forceful wave buffeted the vessel and she was thrown against him. His arm circled her as he braced himself to keep them both from falling. In spite of the growing fear that they would be capsized, Emma was acutely aware of the sturdy column of his leg and pressure of his hand at her waist. Then the sea seemed to have been forgotten as his presence filled her senses. A rush of heated excitement swept through her.

"Guess I wasn't paying as much attention to where I was going as I should have been," he said gruffly, beginning to maneuver the *Reliable Lady* back toward land.

"You did seem to be a bit preoccupied," she managed to reply and marveled that she'd put together a coherent sentence. She was having a very difficult time concentrating. Her body was being jostled against his by the motion of the boat and even the frigid wind could not quench the heat building within her.

"Go down into the cabin," he ordered. "I don't want to have to worry about you getting washed overboard while I get us back to the dock."

The thought of being released brought a rush of disappointment. A protest started to form on her lips, then realizing she was not only being irrational, but she was also hampering his ability to get them safely home, she nodded.

He loosened his hold slowly to make certain she didn't fall, then watched as she made her way down the ladder and into the cabin.

Alone, out of his view, Emma drew a steadying breath. Just remembering the sturdy feel of his body caused her blood to race. "I will not be attracted to a man who makes his living on a boat on the ocean," she stated emphatically, repeating a vow she'd made to herself years earlier.

Determined not to think about her wanton reactions to Mike Flint, she looked out at the sky. Night was falling fast. As the pitching lessened and she saw the marina coming into view, she went back on deck. But she did not return to the bridge. Instead she again seated herself in the fisherman's chair and waited until she could be useful.

When he guided the *Reliable Lady* into its mooring, she jumped out onto the pier and began securing the ropes. After the boat was securely moored and he didn't join her, she'd climbed back on board. She found him in the cabin, making a pot of coffee.

"You should go home and get some rest," she said sternly.

He hadn't looked at her. Instead he kept his attention on his task. "I can't go back there tonight. There are too many memories."

Emma was about to point out that, considering the amount of time he and his grandfather spent on the water, the *Reliable Lady* should be filled with even more memories than the house, but she bit back the words. "A man's boat is like a good friend who provides silent companionship at times when it's needed," she repeated aloud something she recalled her father saying on several occasions.

"Something like that, I guess," Mike replied.

"And the motion of the sea is like being rocked in your mother's arms," she said, completing her father's description.

This time Mike turned to her, a dry expression on his face. "That's taking poetic license a bit too far."

"I was just quoting my father," she replied.

Unexpectedly a crooked grin tilted one corner of his mouth. "That does sound like Peter."

The lopsided smile caused her heart to seem to lurch. Mike Flint could be a very appealing-looking man, she admitted. However, he didn't appeal to her, she added quickly. The need to escape grew strong. She told herself he would be fine on his own. He had his boat and the sea. But she could not make herself leave.

"I could use a cup of hot coffee myself," she said, seating herself at the galley table. The heat from the stove was radiating a small amount of warmth into the cabin, but the chill remained in the air. As he sank onto the padded bench opposite her to wait for the coffee to brew, she frowned at him. "You can't sleep here. You'll freeze."

He shrugged as if her objection was groundless. "I've got plenty of blankets."

His stubbornness caused her own jaw to harden with resolve. "Good, because I'm going to need at least ten," she returned.

He frowned impatiently. "There's no reason for you to stay." Self-consciousness played across his features. "I know it was foolish of me to go on the ocean. I was hurting. I thought being surrounded by open water would help. But I realize now that was a dangerous error in judgment. I want to mourn my grandfather, not join him."

"I'm glad to hear that." A shiver shook her and she pulled her coat more tightly around herself once again. "So how about if we have that cup of coffee and then go back to your place so we don't both catch pneumonia?"

For a moment he looked as if he was again going to reject her suggestion, then unexpectedly he leaned toward her for a closer look. "Your lips are turning a curious shade of blue," he said, a gruff gentleness entering his voice. Lightly he ran his thumb across them as if testing the feel of them.

His touch was warm and the urge to taste his thumb was strong. As if this was the most natural thought in the world, her lips parted slightly awaiting any further exploration he might consider.

He leaned even closer. "I've always been intrigued by those green eyes of yours."

She knew he was going to kiss her and she had no will to pull away. His breath warmed her skin. It was as if the rest of the world had faded into nothingness and only she and he remained. She began to lean in his direction to aid him in his quest.

"Permission to come aboard!" A familiar bellow split the air.

Emma jerked back as the spell was broken.

"Seems as if your father isn't going to wait for any invitation, either," Mike said, easing back into his seat with a resigned sigh as heavy footfalls sounded on the deck.

"Thought I'd go by your place and take over the watch for Emma," Peter said, descending the ladder into the cabin. "When I didn't see her car there, I figured you two'd be here." He gave an exaggerated shiver. "Mighty cold."

Mike eased himself off the bench. "Emma has convinced me that spending the night out here would be foolish."

Peter smiled with pride. "The girl's got a practical head on her shoulders."

But I do have my moments of weakness, Emma thought, shaken by how close she'd come to kissing Mike Flint. The cabin suddenly seemed much too confining. "My toes are beginning to feel like tiny icicles. How about if we leave for Mike's house now," she suggested forcefully.

"Good idea," her father agreed, already heading back up the ladder.

Mike glanced at her and she had a momentary vision of him massaging the warmth back into her feet as they sat in his living room in front of the fireplace. Quickly she scooted off her bench and followed her father outside, leaving Mike to turn off the stove and lights.

On deck, the cold, salty air whipped around her but she barely noticed. She could not believe the reactions she was having...not after all the talks she'd had with herself about never falling for a sailor. "I'll be in my car," she told her father and quickly disembarked.

From the shelter of her vehicle she watched her father and Mike walking up the pier to the parking area. "They're cut from the same cloth," she reminded herself curtly, and again affirmed that she had no intention of getting involved with a duplicate of her father.

Back at Mike's house, she busied herself in the kitchen making sandwiches and coffee while the men built a fire in the fireplace in the living room. But she only prepared two plates. The moments of weakness she'd been experiencing this night had her unnerved. She wanted to get away from this house and Mike Flint as quickly as possible.

As she worked, she assured herself he would be fine now. He had her father as a companion. She carried the food into the living room, set it on the coffee table, announced that she was turning over the watch to her father and bid them both a good-night.

But when she paused in the hall to pull her coat on, Mike came out to join her.

"Thanks," he said. "I guess being alone wasn't such a good idea after all."

There was a warmth in his eyes that again made her toes want to curl. "You're welcome," she'd replied and quickly escaped.

The next evening he'd showed up at her home with a bouquet of flowers. "I was wondering if you'd have dinner with me this Saturday," he'd asked as he handed them to her.

The urge to accept had been strong but she'd spent the day steeling herself against their next encounter. "I think it would be best if we went our separate ways," she'd said.

He'd frowned in confusion and surprise. "That wasn't the impression I got last night."

"I refuse to become involved with a man who is already wed to his boat and the sea," she elaborated bluntly.

"I wouldn't exactly say I was *wed* to either."

She regarded him challengingly. "Giving up the *Reliable Lady* or any of the time you spend on the water, would be like giving up a part of yourself... a part you would not be happy without, right?"

He scowled impatiently as if she was being unreasonable. "That's how I make my living."

"It's your whole life," she corrected. "And not only do you have a charter boat but you have that salvage rig as well. I know that keeping your businesses running must require you to be gone for days at a time. And, when you are in port, you're either repairing or swabbing the *Reliable Lady* or working on your salvage rig, right?"

"I do spend some time on shore but you're basically right," he conceded.

"Of course I'm right," she snapped. Her expression hardened. "Well, I want a man who will have time for me."

The blue of his eyes deepened. "I can promise you, I'd make time for you."

The way he was looking at her caused her will to weaken. "I refuse to spend nights pacing the floor like my mother did when an unexpected storm would blow up the coast and my father was still out on the water," she spat out, more to remind herself of her reasons for her decision than to educate him. "I want a home and a family and a husband who is there to share them with me. I do not want a man who blows in and out like an uncertain wind."

He was regarding her with a shuttered expression now. "You seem to have thought this out pretty thoroughly."

Against her will, the remembered touch of his thumb on her lips caused her legs to feel shaky. Her back stiffened with resolve. "I have."

"Then I wish you luck," he'd said and left.

And so for the past six years, they'd avoided each other whenever possible.

"Mike Flint does not belong on my mind," she admonished herself and forced the images of the past back into the shadows.

Setting aside her plate, she leaned back into the pillows. The September sun had heated the day. Now a gentle breeze was cooling the night to a comfortable warmth. It stirred her hair and a laziness enveloped her.

She closed her eyes and forced her thoughts to Kenneth. He was a much better choice than Mike Flint, she declared, then scowled at herself for allowing the charter boat captain to reenter her mind.

The sound of a vehicle pulling up in front of her house was a welcome interruption.

Had Kenneth decided to cancel his dinner engagement and come back and spend the evening with her after all? she wondered. A smile of welcome began to tilt the corners of her mouth as she opened her eyes and sat up. Immediately the smile vanished. It was Mike Flint coming up her walk.

He mounted the steps to the porch, then approaching the swing, extended a bakery box toward her. "It's a piece of lemon meringue pie from Peg's Diner," he said. "Nearly every time I've seen you in there, you've ordered it."

Emma hid her surprise that he'd noticed what she ate. She'd been sure he'd paid as little attention to her as she'd paid to him. On the other hand, she admitted that she had noticed he always ordered the chocolate cream pie. Knowledge borne out of idle curiosity, she assured herself. "You really shouldn't have," she replied, refusing to accept the box. She wanted no gifts from Mike Flint. Even a slice of pie.

He frowned. "I'm trying to apologize for tonight. I shouldn't have let Drake in and yelled up to you. I shouldn't have even been here. I was on my way downstairs to leave when he knocked. The front door was open. I knew he'd seen me through the screen door. There didn't seem to be any alternative but to let him in. And I figured you wouldn't appreciate it if I went back upstairs and knocked on your door to let you know he was here." A dryness came over his face. "Of course, I guess I could have simply let him go upstairs and announce himself."

"What you did was fine," she replied stiffly. "There's no reason for you to apologize."

He frowned at the bakery box still in his hand, then set it down on the small patio table nearby. Emma expected him to leave. Instead he hooked his thumbs into the pockets of his jeans and stood studying her. "Drake did take my being here rather well. I'm a little surprised considering the rumors that have been flying around all day about your late-night visit to my place."

The implication that Kenneth had not behaved like a man who was truly interested in her, rankled Emma. "He came by the bookstore at noon today and I explained I'd stopped by to see you because of my father." She regarded him haughtily. "He trusts me."

His expression became shuttered. "Looks like you've found what you've been looking for," he said, then added an abrupt, "Good night," and left.

"I have found what I'm looking for," Emma affirmed to herself as she watched him drive away. Kenneth was trusting, kind, a pleasant companion and good friend . . . all the qualities she was looking for in a husband.

"Of course, I wouldn't mind a little more passion in our relationship," she admitted, finding herself wishing he'd surprised her and, in spite of her assurance she didn't mind spending the evening alone, found some excuse to escape from his commitment to the Evanses and come back to spend the evening with her.

In the next instant, she berated herself for not being fair. He'd volunteered to stay and she insisted that he go. He's exactly what I've been looking for, she affirmed once again.

Her gaze shifted to the bakery box. Mike Flint was not a threat to her resolve, she assured herself. "And there's no sense in letting a perfectly good piece of pie go to waste," she added, reaching for it. After all, Peg Jones did make the best pies in town.

Chapter Four

Emma studied Kenneth as they left the bookstore and walked toward Clover Street. Two days had passed since he'd arrived at her home to find Mike Flint there. When he'd come to dinner last night, he'd been unusually quiet. Of course, her father had been particularly boisterous, telling stories and being, in general, the life of the party. That was Peter Wynn's way of attempting to make up for the embarrassment he thought he'd caused her.

Usually she didn't mind her father monopolizing the evening. He knew some very entertaining tales and Kenneth normally enjoyed hearing them. But last night she'd noticed Kenneth's eyes seem to glaze over as if his mind was a million miles away and very soon after dinner he'd pleaded a headache and gone home. Watching him leave she'd been certain something was wrong and wished she'd had more of an opportunity to converse with him privately or, at least, turn the conversation to something that would interest him.

When he'd called this morning and asked her to lunch she'd been relieved. Now she would have a chance to find out what was bothering him. Of course they would need to speak to each other for that.

"Nice day," she said, breaking the silence that had fallen between them since they'd left the bookstore.

"Very," he replied and smiled down at her charmingly. "I hope you don't mind going to Peg's Diner. The food's terrific and I'm especially fond of her cherry pie."

Emma was sure his cheerfulness was being forced. She was also a little taken aback by his declared preference for cherry pie. "I could have sworn it was the coconut cream you liked."

He cocked an eyebrow playfully. "That must have been one of your other boyfriends. I've never liked coconut."

Emma flushed. Obviously she wasn't as observant as she thought. Momentarily at a loss as to what to say, she was relieved that they'd reached the diner. Returning a greeting from Katie Jones saved her from having to come up with an excuse for her mistake.

Once we're seated, I'll introduce a fresh topic of conversation, she told herself, and quickly scanned the booths and tables. The clean, homey eatery with its windows facing the main street in town was a gathering place for the locals and usually did a fairly brisk lunchtime business. Today was no exception. Even most of the counter stools were occupied.

"There's a booth by the window," Katie said helpfully.

Emma had been so preoccupied with Kenneth, she'd only given Katie a cursory glance. Now as she turned back to her friend, she noticed that Katie was wearing an apron with Peg's Diner embroidered across the front. "Did your aunt get caught shorthanded again?" she asked sympathetically, knowing Peg always called on her niece when she was in a bind and needed help.

"Just for a couple of hours so I told her I'd fill in," Katie replied. The bell from the kitchen rang indicating someone's meal was ready. "Got to run." Katie handed them each a menu. "I'll be by to take your order in a minute or two."

Reaching the booth, Emma seated herself so she'd be across the table from Kenneth and began looking through the menu. "I don't know why I'm even reading this," she said, again attempting to initiate a conversation. "I know it by heart."

Kenneth smiled absently at her and she wondered if he'd even heard what she'd said or simply realized she'd spoken and felt he should made some sort of response.

The menu was forgotten as she concentrated on coming up with a subtle way to find out what was on his mind. But she'd always been a straightforward person. Hedging a difficulty was not easy for her. This is ridiculous, she mentally berated herself as a headache began to threaten. One of the reasons she was so fond of Kenneth was that she thought of him as a true friend. And friends did not need to be evasive.

Her gaze narrowed on him. "Would you please tell me what is bothering you," she requested. "You've been preoccupied for the past couple of days." A possible cause for his withdrawn behavior had occurred to her. "If you're upset about finding Mike Flint at my house the other night, I wish you'd just say so and get it out in the open." Quickly she added, "Of course there is no reason for you to be upset about that. He was only there because of my father. But just in case you are, I think we should talk about it."

Surprise showed on his face. "I'm not upset about Mike Flint," he assured her. Reaching across the table, he gave her hand a squeeze. "I trust you, remember?"

Emma experienced a twinge of regret and realized that she'd been hoping he might be feeling at least a smidgen of jealousy. I should be flattered that he trusts me so completely, she silently chided herself. Aloud she asked bluntly, "Then what does have you upset?"

He gave her a quizzical look as if to say he hadn't the slightest idea what she was talking about. "I'm not upset about anything."

Emma was about to point out that his behavior of late had been that of someone with something on his mind when Katie came by to take their order. "The special of the day is chicken and dumplings," she informed them.

"Sounds good," both replied in unison.

Kenneth smiled and this time the smile reached his eyes. "Two minds that travel the same path," he said, then, raising a questioning eyebrow toward Emma, added, "Sweetened iced tea?"

She nodded.

"And two sweetened iced teas," he told Katie.

"Be back in a jiff," she replied with a grin and hurried off.

As Katie left, before Emma could again broach the subject of Kenneth's recent preoccupation, he said, "Clearly we have the same tastes in food. And I've noticed we have very similar tastes in many other things.. clothes and furniture for example."

"I guess we do," Emma admitted, startled by this unexpected observation and his sudden full attention.

"And we both want the same things in life... a home, a family," he continued.

Guessing where this was leading, Emma experienced a wave of panic. You're supposed to be thrilled he's getting ready to ask you to marry him, she admonished herself. Still, an uneasiness remained. Then she noticed he'd again become silent. He was looking beyond her to the entrance of the diner.

Glancing over her shoulder she saw that Mike Flint had entered. He was accompanied by Paul Wooly. Paul, a twenty-two-year-old with a wiry build, brown hair and brown eyes, was Mike's first mate and sometimes captained the charter boat when Mike was out on a salvage job. So Kenneth had been lying about not being upset about finding Mike at her home, she mused as the two men made their way to a newly vacated booth.

But when she turned back to Kenneth, she noticed that his gaze was still focused on the entrance of the diner. Glancing back, she saw the redhead who had been in the bookstore a couple of days earlier. The woman had entered just behind Mike and Paul and was still standing by the door. With the two seamen no longer blocking her view, she was scanning the interior of the diner with a slow, steady gaze. Suddenly, she stopped and Emma realized the woman was looking her way. She experienced the most curious sensation as if she were the prey and the huntress had found her. Then the redhead's gaze shifted to a point beyond Emma and locked there.

Kenneth! It was Kenneth the redhead had been scanning the diner for, Emma realized. She turned back to see anger in his eyes…a deep, dark anger. "Do you know the woman who just entered?" she asked, unable to think of a less blunt approach.

But Kenneth made no response. Emma was not even sure he'd heard her. His gaze had remained locked beyond her. She was about to repeat her question when she saw his jaw tense and out of the corner of her eye caught a glimpse of the blue silk dress the redhead was wearing swishing in their direction.

"It's nice to see you again, Kenneth," the woman said, coming to a halt at their table. Coolly she turned to Emma. "I don't believe I introduced myself the other day. I'm Monica McBrady."

"You two have met?" Kenneth demanded sharply.

"I stopped by the bookstore to see how it had been renovated," Monica explained stiffly, her attention returning to him. "I'm thinking of opening a dress shop in town."

"I doubt very much you will find the kind of clientele you seek here," he replied. "I would think Charleston or Atlanta would be more your style."

Emma had to fight to hide her surprise. Kenneth, who was normally polite if not charming to everyone he met, had practically told the redhead she wasn't welcome in Clover.

"Maybe I've changed my style," Monica replied. Her gaze shifted to Emma. "It's been pleasant meeting you, Miss Wynn," she said crisply, then walked on to a table in the rear.

It took a moment for her to realize the fact that, although Emma hadn't had a chance to introduce herself, Monica had known her name. She glanced at Kenneth to find him scowling at the redhead's departing back. "An old acquaintance?" she asked.

He shrugged. "She and her family were members of the last country club I worked for."

"The woman who just stopped to speak to you is the Evanses' houseguest, isn't she?" Katie asked, arriving at that moment with their food.

"Yes," Kenneth replied, a hint of distaste in his voice.

It suddenly dawned on Emma that the day she'd first encountered Monica McBrady had been the day her father had come home drunk and she'd sent Kenneth to the cocktail party at the Evanses' home alone. And, Monica McBrady must have been one of the attendees, she realized.

"I understand she's considering opening a dress shop," Katie continued thoughtfully.

"I wouldn't take anything she says too seriously," Kenneth warned.

Katie looked surprised by the sharpness in his tone and glanced at Emma with a question in her eyes. Emma gave a small shrug to let her know she had no idea why Kenneth was so skeptical of the woman's motives.

Clearly deciding that a retreat was in order, Katie finished setting their food on the table, then said, "I'd better go take her order before she decides the service is too slow,'' and hurried off.

Emma's gaze leveled on Kenneth. "I've never known you to be so critical of anyone. What happened between the two of you?"

"Nothing," he replied with a finality that told her this was not a subject open to discussion. "These dumplings are delicious," he added, obviously determined to turn the conversation to their food.

For a long moment Emma sat studying him indecisively. One of the reasons she was seriously considering him as a possible husband was that she thought he considered her someone he could confide in. "If you should ever decide you need to talk to someone about whatever this 'nothing' is, you know my number," she volunteered.

He looked at her then. Smiling warmly, he reached over and took her hand in his. "You are a woman a man can rely on. You will never know how much that means to me. And please believe me when I tell you there is nothing to tell about me and Ms. McBrady.''

"I've never seen you so agitated by anyone's presence before," she persisted, letting her skepticism of his assurance show on her face.

He gave a small shrug as if to imply she was making a mountain out of a molehill. "I've just had a very busy morning. I guess I'm not in the best of moods."

Emma didn't buy this explanation and was considering possible subtle ways of pursuing her inquiries when he abruptly glanced at his watch. "I've really got to run. I just remembered a lesson I forgot about," he said. "I'll take care of the bill on my way out."

Talk about making a fast escape, Emma thought, watching him leave a tip on the table then quickly slide out of the booth. She half expected him to jog down the aisle. Instead he paused beside her, lifted her chin with his finger and kissed her lightly.

"I'll take you out to dinner tonight to make up for not being able to stay for lunch," he said. Then before she could make any response, he left in search of Katie to take care of the bill.

Watching him, Emma was now certain something was greatly bothering him. Kenneth Drake was a conservative man. It wasn't natural for him to have kissed her so publicly. Her gaze shifted to the table and the nearly full plate of food he'd left behind.

"Aunt Peg is going to be very insulted." Katie's voice broke into Emma thoughts. "She's not used to people not eating her chicken and dumplings."

Emma glanced up to see concern on her friend's face and she knew it wasn't there because of Peg Jones's possible wrath. "Kenneth just remembered an appointment he'd forgotten about," she explained with schooled nonchalance as if his departure was of no consequence.

Katie looked relieved. "I'll box his meal so you can take it with you." Picking up the plate, she added, "He told me to add a piece of banana cream pie to the bill for your dessert. I've never known you to order that. Decide to try a new taste?"

"Make it a slice of lemon, instead," Emma replied.

Katie smiled and nodded, then headed back to the kitchen.

Forking a bit of chicken into her mouth, Emma found herself feeling irritated that Kenneth hadn't remembered what kind of pie she liked. But then she hadn't remembered what kind he liked, either, she reminded herself. And what kind of dessert either of them liked was of no real importance anyway, she fussed at herself, furious that she was even giving this a moment's thought.

But a few minutes later when Katie brought her dessert, she noticed her friend was also carrying a slice of chocolate pie as well. She watched Katie weave her way down the aisle and place the other dessert in front of Mike Flint.

Grudgingly she was forced to admit that, as hard as she tried not to be, she was aware of Mike when he was present. Apparently more aware than she'd realized, she added. That's because I want to be sure to avoid him, she reasoned.

And remembering that he liked chocolate pie was simply a memory quirk...a bit of trivia that had stuck in her mind and was of no consequence. Assuring herself that she felt nothing but indifference toward the charter boat captain, she forked a bite of pie into her mouth and turned her attention to the people and traffic on the street outside.

But as she took another bite, a prickly sensation on the side of her neck caused her to glance in the direction from which the irritation seemed to be coming. Monica McBrady was staring at her. Realizing Emma was looking her way, the redhead abruptly lowered her gaze to her coffee cup.

Emma frowned. That stare had not been the vacant kind of someone whose mind was elsewhere.

There had been purpose on Miss McBrady's face. Just why had the woman come to Clover? Emma wondered. And did her purpose for being here have something to do with Kenneth?

Emma's shoulders squared. Above all else, Kenneth was her friend and a decent man. If the woman had come to cause him trouble, Emma was prepared to stand by his side.

Realizing that she was now the one who was staring, she ordered herself to return her attention to her food. Instead her gaze traveled around the diner. Against her will, it came to rest on Mike Flint. He looked tired and she unexpectedly found herself worrying that he wasn't getting enough rest. He is not my responsibility, she admonished herself and jerked her gaze back to her pie. But the dessert had lost its appeal. It was time for her to be getting back to the bookstore, anyway, she decided and slid out of the booth.

She waved goodbye to Katie from the door, then stepped out into the bright afternoon sunshine. Walking briskly, she was turning onto the path leading up to the front door of Balanski's Bookstore when a familiar male voice said, "It's a shame you have to spend such a lovely afternoon inside."

For a moment she froze, then turned to find Mike Flint standing only a couple of paces behind her.

"I remember when you used to enjoy the salt breeze blowing in your hair." There was a challenge in his eyes daring her to deny this.

"I still do," she admitted.

Approaching her, he traced the line of her jaw with his finger. "Are you absolutely positive about what you want for your future?'' he asked gruffly, his gaze boring into her as if trying to see through to her very soul.

His touch left a trail of heat. For a moment she felt her resolve weakening. Then she remembered the nights her mother had paced the living room floor and all those weekends the two of them had spent alone. "I'm certain about what I don't want," she replied firmly.

"My grandfather used to warn me that many a sailor goes looking for calmer seas only to discover his true peace lies in his home waters," he cautioned.

Emma felt herself being drawn into the blue depths of his eyes. No, her inner voice screamed. Jerking her gaze free, she said dryly, "I would never have pictured you as a philosopher."

He frowned at her retreat. "My grandfather used to also caution me to take a long look at the water before I steered my boat into it. It can be shallower than you think, he'd say, or have a current that carries you where you don't want to go."

Her jaw firmed. "I never behave rashly."

"No, you don't," he conceded grimly. Challenge again showed on his face. "Have you ever considered the possibility you hold your emotions under too much control?"

She scowled at him. "First you caution me to be careful and now you're suggesting I throw caution to the wind. You can't have it both ways."

He drew a harsh breath as if giving up a struggle he'd been having with himself. "As long as that wind steers you in my direction, I can." Placing his finger under her chin, he tilted her face upward and kissed her lightly. "I've tried to respect your wishes, but I can't sit back and allow Drake to win you without putting up a fight."

Before she could think of anything to say, he'd turned and was walking back to Clover Street. Like no other kiss she'd ever experienced, the heat of his lips continued to linger on hers almost as if the contact still remained. Her heart was pounding and her toes seemed to want to curl with pleasure.

"I'm just in shock," she reasoned curtly under her breath. "I never expected to be kissed by Mike Flint and I most certainly did not expect to be pursued by him." She rubbed her hand across her mouth to brush off the remaining feel of him. "However, he will never catch me."

Having had this little talk with herself, she strode into the bookstore.

"Well, now," Mrs. Balanski greeted her with interest. "I know these old eyes of mine are getting a mite weak but I could have sworn that was Mike Flint out there with you and that he kissed you practically on my front stoop."

"It was nothing," Emma said firmly. A plea entered her voice. "And I'd really appreciate it if you didn't mention this to anyone. I didn't invite it and I can guarantee it will never happen again."

A mischievous gleam sparkled in Martha's eyes. "A touch of jealousy has made many a man pop the question a lot faster. It couldn't hurt for Kenneth to know you have someone else who's interested in you."

Emma shook her head. "I don't want jealousy to be the spark that ignites a proposal. And I don't want my name even linked with Mike Flint."

Martha frowned thoughtfully. "I don't understand your attitude toward him. I've always liked him. He's an honest, hardworking man." She suddenly grinned. "And he has that attractive dimple in his left cheek when he smiles."

That dimple did add a certain intriguing rakishness to his appearance, Emma conceded silently, then was furious with herself for this admission. "He simply doesn't appeal to me," she replied.

Martha shrugged as if to say she'd tried to be helpful. "When I was a girl, we enjoyed having several suitors and flirting outrageously. It added excitement to the chase, so to speak."

"I prefer a comfortable courtship," Emma returned. But as she continued on to the back room to put her purse away she found herself thinking that she did sound a bit dull. "*Practical* is what I am," she said, defending herself under her breath.

Chapter Five

As she turned from the stove to put the steak she'd just broiled for her father on the table, Emma grinned crookedly at the prettily wrapped package sitting at her usual place. She'd been expecting it.

"Just a little something to let you know how sorry I am for the other night and for being such a bore last night," her father said with deep apology and remorse.

There was no denying the genuineness of his repentance. Even if she had been angry with him, she knew she would have forgiven him. She always did. "I understand about the other night and you weren't a bore last night," she assured him.

He didn't look convinced. "Seemed to me Kenneth left a mite early."

"He was just tired," she replied, adding a baked potato to her father's plate.

"Then you two are getting along all right?"

Emma glanced at her father as she sat down in her chair to unwrap her package. She could have sworn there was a hint of hope in his voice that she and Kenneth weren't getting along. "We're getting along just fine."

"Glad to hear that." He quickly dropped his eyes to his steak and cut a piece but not before Emma glimpsed a touch of disappointment on his face.

"I thought you liked Kenneth."

He met her gaze. "I do," he assured her.

Emma knew her father well. There was something he wasn't saying. "But...?" she prompted.

"It's just that I noticed Mike Flint watching you a couple of weeks back when I'd forgotten my lunch and you brought it to the marina. It was the kind of look a man gets when he's interested in a woman."

Emma could barely believe her ears. Her father was matchmaking! "I am not interested in Mike Flint," she said firmly.

"You're not interested in marrying a seafaring man," he corrected.

A flush of embarrassment colored Emma's cheeks. Through the years, she'd worked hard to keep her father from guessing she felt this way. She'd never wanted to hurt his feelings.

"I asked Mike why he didn't come courting," he said, letting her know it was useless to try to lie her way out.

"I simply prefer a man whose fate isn't dependent on the shifts of the wind and the currents in the sea," she replied honestly.

Concern suddenly etched itself deeply into his features. "Was your mother unhappy with the life I provided her?"

"No." Rising from the table, she went to his chair and gave him a hug. "You made her very happy. I don't know of any couple who was more in love. I envy you that."

He drew a satisfied breath. "Your mother was a special woman." He gave her hand a pat as she released him. "You're a special woman, too."

"Thanks." She breathed a sigh of relief to see the concern gone from his face. Returning to her chair, she again began to open the package.

"Mike Flint's a good man...a steady man," he said, forking another bite.

Emma looked up at him with a frown that let him know she thought they'd finished with this subject.

"'Course Kenneth is a good man, too," he added quickly. "Either one would make a fine husband."

Emma merely shook her head at his continued effort to champion Mike, then concentrated on opening the package while he completed carrying the bite to his mouth.

Inside the prettily wrapped box was a miniature porcelain doll dressed in an elaborate ball gown.

Peter smiled lovingly at his daughter. "She reminded me of you when you got all decked out in that antebellum dress for the Fourth of July celebration at the country club."

Emma returned his smile. "She's lovely." Then rising from the table, she added, "I'd better finish getting myself ready. Kenneth should be here any minute."

"Have a good time," he said as she headed to the door.

Pausing, she turned back. "Thanks, I will."

A sheepish expression came over his face. "I told Mike that if I was in his shoes I wouldn't give up too quickly trying to win you. I told him you were worth fighting for."

Emma shook her head in frustration. "Thanks, Dad," she returned dryly, and completed her exit.

"I'm just performing my fatherly duties to the best of my ability," he called after her. "Wouldn't want you to miss an opportunity you might regret."

First Martha and now her father, she groaned as she went upstairs. Well, no one was going to undermine her resolve. She knew what kind of life she wanted.

And Kenneth was her Mr. Right, she assured herself a few minutes later as she climbed into the passenger seat of his Mustang.

Sliding in on the driver's side, he smiled at her. "I thought we'd skip the barbecue at the country club and have a quiet dinner at my place."

"That sounds nice," she replied, noting that the smile did not quite reach his eyes. There was also a rigid set to his jaw she'd only seen when he was holding back anger. "And maybe you'll finally tell me what has been bothering you," she added bluntly.

He raised an eyebrow questioningly as if he had no idea what she was talking about. "Like I've already told you, nothing is bothering me."

"That would be more believable if you hadn't said it through almost clenched teeth," she returned.

He frowned at the road ahead. "You're exaggerating."

The fact that he hadn't looked at her made Emma positive there was something seriously wrong. "One of the things I value most in our relationship is that we've always been honest with each other," she said frankly. "Above all else, I'm your friend. You can count on me." She studied the taut line of his jaw. "Is Monica McBrady here to cause you trouble?"

His jaw twitched in an outward display of irritation. Emma was sure he was angry with her for being so persistent, then he said curtly, "Monica is merely a thorn in my side. She can't cause me any trouble." The way he spoke let Emma know that all of his ire was directed at the redhead.

Even more, she was now certain this "nothing" was much more serious than he was admitting. She wanted to help but first she had to know what was going on. "Who is Monica McBrady? What is she to you?"

Kenneth was now glowering at the road ahead. "She's an old girlfriend." Self-mockery showed on his face. "Actually I once thought I was in love with her. But I was wrong."

A sudden truth dawned on Emma. Monica was a guest of the Evanses. That meant she had free access to the country club. "Are we having dinner at your place because you honestly want to spend some time alone with me or because you want to avoid Monica?"

He glanced toward her then and smiled one of his most charming smiles. "I want to spend a quiet evening with you."

Emma didn't know exactly why, he certainly sounded truthful, but she didn't totally believe him.

I'm just looking for trouble where there isn't any, she scolded herself a little later as she carried two place settings out to the table on the balcony of Kenneth's condominium. They'd stopped by the video rental store on their way here and picked up a couple of Cary Grant classics. By the time they'd reached the condo, Kenneth had begun to honestly relax and was telling her an amusing story about one of the lessons he'd given that day. Now Frank Sinatra was playing on the stereo while the coals in the barbecue were heating and Kenneth was creating a salad he swore would rival those of the great chefs of Europe.

"The perfect salad," he announced, joining her and placing the huge bowl of cut greens on the table with a flourish.

"The perfect beginning of a perfect dinner on a perfect evening," she replied. Breathing in deeply of the warm summer air, she gazed out toward the ocean. "Beautiful scenery... a charming dinner companion... what more could a girl ask for?" This was exactly what she wanted her life to be like, she added silently. Deep within a tiny note of discord twanged. She ignored it.

"Absolutely nothing, I hope," he replied, drawing her into his arms.

As his lips found hers, she waited for her toes to want to curl. They didn't. She added her own energy to the kiss. Still, nothing. Not *nothing,* she berated herself. His touch was pleasant, his lips warm and the kiss was nice. And that's enough for me, she affirmed.

"Dinner could wait awhile," he said huskily, nuzzling the hollow behind her ear, then capturing her earlobe gently in his teeth.

Emma stiffened. She wasn't ready for what she knew he was suggesting. "I'd sort of planned on saving some experiences for my wedding night," she said, trying to explain her reticence as much to herself as to him. In a forced playful tone, she added, "Besides, I wouldn't want the greatest salad in the world to wilt before we had a chance to eat it."

Kenneth breathed a resigned sigh. Then lifting his head from hers, he gave her an understanding wink. "No, we wouldn't."

As she seated herself and watched him put the steaks on the grill before joining her, she frowned at the way she'd recoiled from him. I'm simply more old-fashioned than I thought, she reasoned. And being old-fashioned was not a bad thing. This way her wedding night would be very special. Satisfied with her conclusions as to why she'd reacted as she had, she began serving the salad.

During the meal she worked to keep the conversation light, bringing up old comedy movies she'd especially enjoyed. Again Kenneth's taste and hers seemed to match perfectly. We are so right for each other, she told herself as he insisted she remain seated while he went into the kitchen to get their desserts.

A knock on the door interrupted her thoughts. "I'll get it," she called out, already out of her chair.

Opening the door, she had to fight back a gasp of surprise.

"I didn't want Kenneth to miss having some of Jason's fabulous barbecue," Monica McBrady said, extending a platter toward Emma.

Protectiveness welled within Emma. Whatever this woman's game was, she would not allow her to hurt

Kenneth. "I'm sure he'll enjoy them." She accepted the platter but remained in the doorway, blocking the redhead's entrance.

A flush of embarrassment had begun to spread across Monica's features.

"Who's here?" Kenneth's voice died in an abrupt snort.

Glancing over her shoulder, Emma saw him standing a few feet behind her, an expression of angry impatience on his face.

Monica visibly stiffened. "I thought you were ill. Jason said you'd skipped the barbecue because you weren't feeling well. I apologize for interrupting an obviously romantic evening."

As the redhead turned to make a quick retreat, Emma was stunned by the pain she glimpsed in Monica McBrady's eyes. Closing the door, she turned to Kenneth. He was still glaring beyond her to where Monica had stood.

Uncertain of what to say, she recalled the platter in her hands. "I'll just put this in the kitchen."

He blinked, clearly surprised by the sound of her voice, and she realized he'd momentarily forgotten she was even there. "I'm sorry about the interruption," he apologized gruffly, following her into the kitchen.

"Are you sure you and Monica McBrady don't have some unfinished business?" she asked bluntly, as she put the meat into the refrigerator.

"None," he replied firmly.

"I think she thinks you do."

"Monica changes her mind the way the wind changes direction. Besides, what she wants isn't important. As far as I'm concerned there is no 'unfinished' business between us."

She wanted to believe him, but her instincts warned her this could be foolish. "There seems to be a lot of anger remaining on your part. You wouldn't feel that way if you hadn't felt strongly about her."

"I told you," he growled, "I thought I was in love with her. I suppose I was. But I'm not anymore." His expression and his voice softened. "You've healed me."

Emma regarded him thoughtfully. "Maybe not quite."

"Yes, fully," he insisted. Setting the desserts aside, he approached her and took her in his arms. "You're warm, sweet and a woman a man can count on. That's what I want. Marry me, Emma."

This is what you've been telling yourself you want, she reminded herself. But the word *yes* refused to form. Instead she heard herself saying, "I don't want to feel you're merely asking me on the rebound."

He frowned. "I'm not. It's been over between Monica and me for nearly a year."

"I'm not so sure about that. I'll need a little time to believe you. Ask me again in two weeks," she bargained.

Determination etched itself into his features. "I'll ask you every day if necessary until you agree."

"Two weeks," she repeated.

"Then how about dessert and a movie for now?" he suggested.

Emma nodded. "Sounds like a plan to me." While he retrieved the desserts she called herself a fool. She could lose him. Better to lose him than to marry a man who would spend his life pining over another woman, she rebutted, and every instinct she had agreed.

A short while later as they sat on the balcony eating fresh strawberries and cream, drinking coffee and watching the sunset, Emma glanced over at Kenneth. There was a grim set to his jaw and a vacant look in his eyes as if his mind were a million miles away. "A penny for your thoughts," she said. "Or maybe even a quarter. You look pretty serious."

He jerked his attention to her and she had the impression he'd forgotten she was even there. Then he smiled warmly with apology. "Believe me they are not worth even a penny." Levering himself out of his chair, he reached for her hands and gently pulled her to her feet. "How about watching one of those videos we rented?"

He was being evasive, she was sure. She was also sure that trying to probe would be useless. Besides, she was fairly certain of what was on his mind...or rather who...Monica McBrady. "A movie sounds wonderful," she replied.

An hour and a half later, Emma was studying Kenneth covertly as the ending credits ran across the screen. Again he looked as if his mind was a million miles away. "I think I should be going home," she said, easing herself off the sofa.

He frowned at her. "We have another movie to watch."

She forced a wide yawn. "I'm more tired than I thought and I've got to go to work tomorrow."

"I guess I haven't been very good company tonight," he apologized. Drawing her into his arms, he kissed her. "I promise to be much more attentive in the future."

"As long as you're being honest with me and yourself about your feelings for Monica McBrady, that's all that matters," she replied, wanting to let him know she'd guessed where his mind had been.

His gaze narrowed on her. "I am."

Again she did not entirely believe him, but she allowed the subject to be dropped. Time will tell, she told herself, deciding not to pursue this any further tonight.

"I've arranged for us to play golf with the Evanses this Saturday. Tee off will be at eight," he informed her as he drove her home.

Mentally Emma groaned. She couldn't seem to get the hang of the game. Five times out of ten she sliced the ball into the rough. "You just like to play with me because my handicap's so high and yours is so low," she bantered, attempting to lighten her mood.

He grinned at her. "I like to play with you because you have a cute little way of shifting your hips that distracts not only me but Jason Evans. His game is always at least six strokes off when you're with us."

"Are you sure that isn't because I slow down the game so much his blood pressure goes up and he can't concentrate?" she returned dryly.

He gave her a lecherous look. "Absolutely."

Emma couldn't stop herself from grinning back. Then Jason Evans was forgotten as they turned onto her street and she saw Mike Flint's truck parked in front of her house.

"Looks like you've got company," Kenneth observed with a frown.

"My father has company," she corrected.

As he walked her to her door, she felt her nerves growing tense. "I know this is going to sound impolite, but I'm not going to invite you in," she said with apology. "I want to simply sneak up to my room without seeing my father or Mike. I'm in no mood to get into an argument with either of them tonight."

He smiled softly down at her. "I understand." At her front door, he drew her into his arms for a long, tender good-night kiss then returned to his car.

Rather than going immediately inside, she stood on the porch and waved goodbye as he drove off. Was she making a mistake by not accepting his proposal tonight? she wondered.

"I really wish you'd stop kissing other men."

Emma jerked around to see Mike standing in the doorway. "I will kiss whomever I please."

A glint of amusement showed in his eyes. "You have always had a mind of your own. Granted you are sometimes misguided but then we all make mistakes."

"I am not misguided," she snapped back. His presence made her tense and she decided that retreat would be the smartest path. "If you'll excuse me, I was on my way to my room."

Brushing past him, her shoulder touched his arm. The contact sent a startling surge of heat radiating through her. Quickly she continued toward the stairs.

"A person could get the impression you're running away from me. I never thought you'd behave so cowardly," he chided.

The challenge in his voice brought her to a halt. Her shoulders squared with pride and she turned to face him. "I am not behaving cowardly. I simply have no interest in spending time in your company."

Approaching her, he trailed a finger along the curve of her ear. "If you'd give me a chance, you might find you like my company."

Emma had to fight to keep from gasping as shivers of delight coursed through her. Life with him would be unsettled and lonely, she reminded herself and steeled herself against any further traitorous responses. "I'm sure you can be pleasant, however, I have more important things to do with my time."

Capturing her by the chin, he forced her to look up at him. "Lying to yourself can prove to be the most foolhardy deceit of all," he cautioned.

His touch was disconcerting but she was determined to stand her ground. "I am not lying to myself."

"Tisk. Tisk," he admonished mockingly, letting her know he didn't believe her. His gaze narrowed on hers. "Granted they have been brief, but I'd swear I've seen momentary glimpses of passion for me in your eyes. In fact, one of those glimpses happened just this afternoon right after I kissed you and before you had time to rebuild that icy shield you're so insistent on keeping between us." Before she could respond, his lips found hers.

She ordered herself to pull away but her legs suddenly seemed too weak to move. Her heart pounded violently and her blood raced. Stop this! she screamed at herself.

Then slowly, with a final nibble on her lips as if to say a regretful goodbye, he lifted his head away. A sense of being abandoned swept through her.

"The heat I see in your eyes right now isn't anger," he said in a tone that implied he'd proved his point.

Emma drew a shaky breath. She couldn't deny the effect his kiss had on her. "I'll admit you do have a certain physical appeal," she conceded grudgingly, taking a step back to free herself from his touch. "However, I'm looking for a great deal more in a relationship." Her gaze cooled. "Stay away from me, Mike Flint," she ordered, then turned abruptly and started up the stairs.

"I've got a feeling we would both live to regret it, if I did that," he called out to her retreating back.

Alone in her room, for the second time in less than two weeks, Emma fought back a primordial scream. Why couldn't Kenneth's kiss feel as exciting as Mike Flint's! she fumed. Kenneth was exactly what she'd been waiting for. "Maybe I should find myself a deserted island and live out my days there," she muttered.

Shock spread over her face. That kiss had really unhinged her! She was even thinking like a sailor. "It's just a temporary insanity. If I stay away from the insufferable Mr. Flint I'll be fine," she assured herself.

Chapter Six

The next afternoon, Emma was stocking a bottom shelf when a pair of expensive blue wedgies came into view. Straightening to a standing position, her gaze traveled upward over a designer sundress to Monica McBrady's face.

"I was wondering if I could have a few words with you in private," the redhead said.

It was more of an order than a request and Emma was tempted to refuse. But her curiosity was too strong. "We can go into the stockroom."

Monica nodded her agreement and Emma led the way.

As they entered the room, Monica closed the door, then stood in front of it and faced Emma squarely. "I'm not good at playing games so I'll be blunt. Is Kenneth in love with you and are you in love with him?"

"That's rather a personal question," Emma hedged, feeling uncomfortable about verbally committing either herself or Kenneth.

Monica shrugged. "It doesn't matter. I love Kenneth with all my heart. I foolishly lost him. It was all my fault. I could never quite believe he really loved me. I know I'm not a raving beauty and Kenneth could have his pick of beauties. Also, in the past, there have been men who have courted me just for my money. To make a long story short, because of my experiences in the past, I was suspicious of Kenneth's motives for asking me out, but he was persistent and I was too attracted to resist. We started seeing each other and I fell head over heels in love with him."

Monica drew a terse breath, then continued. "My father liked Kenneth and offered him a partnership in a private golf club. But I didn't see it for what it was...a simple business deal that would be profitable to both of them. I saw it as my father buying a husband for me. After I broke off with Kenneth, my father still wanted to go through with the deal but Kenneth not only refused, he left town. That was when I realized I'd made a mistake. I tried to patch things up but Kenneth refused to have anything to do with me. He said I hadn't trusted him then and, therefore, he couldn't count on me to trust him in the future. I thought getting back with him was hopeless and it may be. But I haven't been able to forget him."

Determination etched itself into Monica's features. "I want him back and I'm going to do everything in my power to achieve that goal."

"And what if Kenneth doesn't want to come back to you?" Emma asked.

"I want him to be happy," the redhead said stiffly. "If I have truly killed the feelings he once had for me and he is now honestly in love with you, then I'll wish you both well and leave."

Emma was certain Monica was fighting back tears. "I also want Kenneth to be happy. And I don't want to marry a man who is in love with another woman." She held out her hand. "I appreciate your honesty."

Monica accepted the handshake. "Thus the gauntlet is cast," she said. Then without a further word, she turned and left.

Sinking into one of the chairs, Emma stared out the window at the garden beyond. If she lost Kenneth she'd probably regret it for the rest of her life, she warned herself. But if she married him and he was truly in love with the redhead, all three of them would live to regret it.

Emma sat on a bench outside the clubhouse staring at the flower bed on the other side of the brick path. Saturday morning had arrived. Golf was definitely not her game and she'd hoped for rain. However, her wishes had not been answered. The sky was clear and sunny.

"What a gorgeous day for a round of golf." A female voice broke into Emma's thoughts.

Turning in the direction from which the words of greeting had come, Emma saw that Carla Evans had joined her. Emma knew Carla was sixty but the woman could easily pass for forty. Through the miracles provided in the most expensive beauty salons, her hair was still a soft honey blond and her complexion retained the peaches-and-cream glow of a twenty-year-old. A face-lift or perhaps two had erased the wrinkles time had brought, and her daily exercise routine kept her figure trim. She was probably in better shape than a great many women half her age, Emma mused as she forced a smile. "Yes, a glorious day."

Interest showed in the older woman's eyes. "I understand Kenneth is negotiating with Jason for a long-term contract to manage the pro shop. That sounds like a man who is definitely putting down roots."

"And we couldn't ask for a finer addition to our community." Jason Evans's voice boomed from behind his wife.

Emma looked beyond Carla to see the short, slightly plump sixty-five-year-old man approaching them. Most of his hair was gone leaving only a white fringe around the edges, but that seemed only to add more dignity to his upper-class bearing. Kenneth was with him and both were smiling.

"You two look like a couple of men who have cut a deal," Carla remarked happily.

Jason's grin broadened. "I believe we have and I'm sure the board will go along with my recommendation. We all want to keep Kenneth here in Clover."

"Congratulations," Emma said, as Kenneth joined her and offered his hand to help her up from the bench. She knew this contract meant a great deal to him and the gleam of satisfaction in his eyes was further proof he was pleased with whatever terms had been agreed upon.

His gaze leveled on her. "This deal will be important to both of us."

I am being stupid about hesitating to accept his offer of marriage, she admonished herself as he smiled warmly at her. He was charming, an understanding friend and comfortable to be with. And he wanted the same things in life that she wanted. What more could she ask for?

Smiling back, she noticed his attention abruptly shift to a point beyond her and a glint of anger showed in his eyes. Glancing over her shoulder, she saw Monica approaching.

"I thought I'd drop by the clubhouse and see if anyone needs a fourth," the redhead said, joining the group.

Monica McBrady was a very good reason for hesitating, Emma reminded herself. "Why don't you take my place," she heard herself saying. "I've really never been able to get the hang of this game."

Kenneth turned his glare to her. "I'm sure Monica can find another foursome."

Monica looked confused while Jason and Carla exchanged glances that suggested they realized they weren't aware of all that was going on.

Emma met Kenneth's glare with resolve. "I really have a splitting headache. I was hoping it would go away but it seems to be getting worse."

Kenneth's gaze softened as enlightenment dawned on him. Clearly he'd guessed her ploy. "I will miss your company. However, if you insist on giving your spot to Monica, it makes no difference to me. I'll be by at six to pick you up for dinner."

Before she could change her mind, Emma quickly bid the others goodbye and left. Walking to her car, she couldn't believe she'd practically thrown Kenneth at Monica. I'm merely being practical, she told herself. Forcing the two of them together was the only way she could be certain he was being honest with himself as well as with her. If Monica truly meant nothing to him, then playing a round of golf with her couldn't hurt.

"Or he could discover his feelings haven't died and I could lose him," she reminded herself. "If that is the case, I'd lose him eventually anyway," she added philosophically. The thought that she should be a little more anxious about the outcome to this day occurred to her. I'm simply being practical, she told herself again.

Driving away from the country club, she meant to go home. Instead, the clear, sunny day beckoned her to remain outdoors and she drove to the marina. Hoping her father hadn't yet left with his charter for the day, she parked and walked briskly to his slip. The *Nancy Belle* was gone. Standing there, gazing out over the water, she frowned. She really had wanted to be out there today... to feel the breeze in her hair and smell the salt air.

"Is there a problem? Do you need for me to radio your father?" a familiar male voice asked from behind her.

Silently she groaned. She hadn't considered the possibility of encountering Mike Flint. "No, there's no problem," she said, turning to him.

He regarded her thoughtfully. "You were looking very wistful. It couldn't be that you came down here hoping to go sailing with him?"

She frowned impatiently. "I never said I didn't enjoy going out for a day's sailing or fishing."

A grin spread over his face. "Then you can come with me. I could use extra crew to help with my charter. It's a couple with two kids. I'd feel better with another hand on board to make sure we don't lose anyone overboard."

His smile was inviting and Emma found herself tempted. Warning signals flashed in her brain. "Thanks, but no thanks."

His gaze traveled appraisingly over her. "If you're worried about getting those dressy slacks and that sweater ruined, I'll reimburse you for any damage."

Emma was shaken. His inspection had been quick and done without even the hint of a leer in his eyes, yet she'd felt his gaze almost like a physical touch. "I really don't want to go," she said firmly. Get out of here, her inner voice ordered, and she started to walk away.

His hand closed around her arm, preventing her from escaping. "You are afraid of spending a little time with me, even in the presence of others, aren't you?" he challenged.

"Don't be ridiculous," she snapped, attempting to ignore the heat of his touch and the way it was causing a curl of excitement to weave its way through her.

"Good, then you can crew for me." His hold tightened and he began guiding her toward the *Reliable Lady*. "I've got a clean shirt on board you can put on in place of that sweater. It will hang long enough, it should save your slacks from too much harm."

"I am not going out with you," she stated firmly again, attempting to pull away.

He stopped and faced her. "You can't run away from me forever."

"I am not running away from you!"

"Prove it." Releasing her, he nodded toward his boat.

Get away from here as fast as you can, her inner voice ordered, but pride held her back. She would not run like a scared rabbit. "Fine. I'll crew for you."

He smiled with triumph. "You get to bait the hooks," he said, waving her on ahead of him.

Well, I did want to smell the sea breezes today, she told herself. And she could keep busy and ignore him.

"Ahoy, Captain." A man's voice rang out from the parking area.

Emma looked in the direction from which the shout had come to see a couple with two children, a boy who looked to be around twelve and a girl who looked to be a year or two younger, waving to Mike.

"Ahoy," he called back.

"Permission to come aboard?" the man yelled cheerfully, making his way to the pier with both children in tow while his wife followed behind.

The woman looked a little uneasy, Emma noticed.

"My wife has trouble with seasickness," the man said when he reached Mike. "She thinks it would be best if she didn't come along."

"Are you sure you can keep an eye on the children?" the woman asked anxiously as she came to a halt beside her husband and looked up at him with concern. "Maybe I should keep them with me."

"We want to go on the boat," the boy insisted with an impatience in his voice that implied he did not consider himself a child.

"We'll be careful and not lean over the side," the little girl pleaded, her hold on her father's hand tightening.

"If it will ease your mind, I've hired extra crew for the day," Mike interjected, indicating Emma with a nod of his head. "We'll keep a close eye on them."

Realizing that Emma was going along, the woman visibly relaxed. After only a moment more of hesitation, she nodded her consent. "Have fun," she said, giving each of the children hugs. "And obey the captain, your father and the nice lady." Straightening, her gaze leveled on Mike. "You'll make sure they wear life preservers at all times."

"I'll fasten them on myself," he promised.

Anxiousness again appeared on the woman's face as she turned back to the children. "And don't take them off," she ordered.

"We won't," they promised in unison.

"I'm Don and this is George and Andrea," the man introduced himself and the children to Emma.

"I'm pleased to meet you," she replied, relieved to have the added responsibility of the children. With their care constantly on her mind, she could easily forget about Mike being there.

"Now that all our problems are solved, shall we be on our way?" Mike suggested, in a tone that was more of a command than a question.

"Absolutely," the man replied, giving the children a slight shove forward. "Before their mother changes her mind."

Both children nodded in agreement and quickly followed Mike down the pier.

Reaching the *Reliable Lady* ahead of the rest, Mike called to Paul to toss him three life preservers. "I always keep my word to a lady," he said as the others reached him. Catching the vests, he extended the adult-size one to the father. "You'll have to put these on before you come aboard," he insisted, his voice taking on the brisk edge of authority.

Handing one of the child-size ones to Emma for the little girl, he added, "There's one in the cabin you can put on when you change into that shirt I promised."

He then turned his attention to the boy. In spite of the child's promise to his mother, Emma saw the momentary expression of protest on George's face when his gaze fell on the third vest still in Mike's hand. Then she saw Mike give him a stern look and the boy cooperated fully as the vest was slipped on him.

As the little girl began to squirm into her vest, Emma noticed that the child was not really paying attention. Instead, Andrea was peering around her at Mike with an expression that was somewhere between awe and fear. Well, the blond-haired seaman could be intimidating, especially when he was captaining his boat, Emma conceded. Further proof of this came when she glanced over her shoulder to discover that the father had pulled his vest on hastily and was standing stiffly awaiting the next order.

Well, Mike Flint might be able to easily bend others to his will, but he wasn't going to bend her, she affirmed.

After helping their passengers on board, Emma descended into the cabin. Following Mike's instructions, she found the shirt he'd promised. As she slipped into it, she experienced a curiously stimulating sensation. It was almost as if she was being enveloped in the owner's arms. A rush of heated excitement raced through her. "It's just a shirt and I'm not interested in its owner," she snapped under her breath, using the sound of her voice to make this official and binding. Grabbing her life jacket, she pulled it on as she joined the others on deck.

The father and his children were already strapped into the fishermen's chairs.

"It would be safest if all of you stay seated until we get to where we'll be fishing," Mike was saying.

His tone was polite but Emma noticed all three nodding as if they'd just received a command they knew better than to disobey.

Recalling how they'd all scurried into their vests as well, she frowned. Not only was Mike Flint wedded to the sea, but he was also obviously a natural authoritarian. And the last thing she wanted in a husband was a man who ruled his home with an iron fist and whose children cowered from him. Shocked that she'd used Mike Flint and husband in the same thought, she scowled at herself and took a seat beside the young girl so she could watch over her.

Mike gave her an approving nod and she realized he'd wanted her to oversee the child. That she'd pleased him caused an unexpected surge of pleasure. I'm merely delighted to have preguessed him, she told herself and concentrated on the passengers and the beauty of the day.

Joining Paul on the bridge, Mike guided the *Reliable Lady* out onto the open sea. There, the wind was stronger and waves rocked the vessel. Emma noticed

Andrea beginning to pale. "Don't look at the water," she instructed. "Look up at the sky or the horizon."

The child nodded and shifted her line of vision.

But even when the wind died and the sea grew calmer, Emma noticed that the paleness of Andrea's complexion remained.

"Time to bait the hooks," Mike called down from the bridge, cutting the engine and turning the wheel over to Paul.

Emma rose and began distributing the poles. Reaching the deck, Mike headed to the bait bucket and opened it. As he took out a squid and approached Andrea to bait her line, the girl's face turned ashen.

"I don't feel so well," she said. The last word was slurred by bile rising in her throat, then she buckled over.

Mike's expression changed from a smile to a look of horror. He took a step back but not quickly nor far enough. The contents of Andrea's stomach spilled out onto his shoes and splashed up onto the legs of his jeans.

"Mom warned you not to eat chocolate cake for breakfast this morning," her brother spoke up, reprimandingly.

"I'm really sorry about this," the father apologized, starting to unbuckle his seat belt and rise from his chair, clearly expecting to have to protect his child from Mike's wrath.

Andrea had finished being sick; now tears were rolling down her cheeks as she looked with fear at the captain of the boat.

Mike abruptly grinned and winked. "Even the best sailors get seasick once in a while." He put a hand up to the father to indicate there was no reason for him to leave his seat, then turning to Emma, he said, "Maybe you should take Andrea into the cabin and clean her up a little."

Emma had been studying him for some sign of hidden anger. To her surprise, there was none. But as she guided the child into the cabin, she did look back in time to see a fleeting expression of discomfort on his features. Then he was all business as he baited the father's and son's hooks.

When she and Andrea returned to the deck a few minutes later, Emma was surprised to discover it had already been swabbed. Looking for Mike, she saw him standing at the railing pulling up a fresh bucket of seawater. He lifted his foot and lower leg over the rail and poured the water over his shoe and pants leg.

"I'm really sorry," Andrea said to her in a whisper, watching the sea captain with rounded eyes, clearly still afraid Mike's temper might suddenly flare.

"I'm sure you're not the first to have an accident like that," Emma soothed. "Do you think you're ready to do some fishing?"

Andrea glanced toward the bait bucket skeptically.

"Remember, whoever catches the biggest fish gets to choose the movie we go see tomorrow," her father said encouragingly.

"You don't have to look while I bait your hook. And I'll cast your line for you," Emma offered.

"The captain said there were some really big groupers caught in these waters yesterday," Andrea's brother coaxed.

The girl shrugged, then nodded to Emma.

Glancing starboard as she lifted the lid of the bait bucket, Emma saw Mike pulling up another bucket of water and rinsing off his other foot. There was still no anger on his face.

Returning her attention to Andrea, Emma placed her body between the hook she was baiting and the child's line of vision. No sense in tempting fate a second time, she'd decided. Then she cast the line and handed the pole to the child.

"Feeling better?" Mike asked, coming to stand beside Andrea.

She glanced up at him as if still not certain he wasn't angry. "Yes, thank you."

He grinned and winked again. "I've got some crackers in case you get to feeling queasy again."

Andrea visibly relaxed. "Thanks," she said, then turned her attention to her line.

Emma had backed far enough away so that she could watch all three charters easily. As Mike joined her, silently she conceded that her description of him ruling his home with an iron fist had been overly judgmental. Aloud, she heard herself admitting, "You handled that well."

"I consider it good practice for fatherhood," he replied.

She glanced up at him to see him watching her with his jaw set in a purposeful line.

"I think two would be nice," he continued.

To her chagrin, she found herself picturing two little boys, one with her black hair and green eyes and one with Mike's blond hair and blue eyes, standing on either side of him. Both were dressed in jeans, sweatshirts and sneakers like their father. Two more males whose hearts would belong to the sea, she thought with a groan. Angry with herself for even conjuring up the image, she met his gaze with a determination of her own. "I hope you and your future wife are happy. Be sure to send me an invitation to the wedding."

Leaning down as if to whisper in her ear, he kissed the side of her neck instead. "It wouldn't be a wedding without you," he said. Then straightening, he strode to the chair where Andrea was sitting, a pout of boredom beginning to form on her face.

Emma stood frozen while goose bumps rose and tendrils of excitement wove through her. All right! All right! Hadn't she already admitted that she found Mike Flint physically attractive? But that was as far as her feelings went or would ever go, she affirmed.

And so what if Kenneth didn't cause her body to respond so...actively? As long as he was truly over Monica McBrady, he was the perfect husband for her, and she did care for him. Besides, the kind of passion Mike elicited couldn't last forever. Having had this little talk with herself, she assured herself she was once again in total control of her world.

She did, however, keep as much distance as possible between herself and the blond-haired sea captain for the rest of the afternoon.

By the time they docked, she was exhausted. To everyone's relief Andrea's stomach had remained calm during the remainder of the day in spite of the fact that she'd drunk half a dozen sodas and eaten heartily of the lunch Mike had provided. As they disembarked the little girl was smiling proudly. To both her father's and her brother's chagrin, she'd caught the biggest fish.

"And there goes another example of how a bad start can turn into a triumphant finish," Mike said, coming to stand beside Emma and wave goodbye to their charters.

As she glanced up at him, he caught her chin in his hand. "And I have every confidence we will finish as well," he added, then placed a light kiss on her lips.

Emma's legs weakened and the urge to sway into his arms was strong. Abruptly she took a step back. "We are finished," she said firmly.

Like a physical touch, she could feel his eyes on her as she turned and walked away.

"Looks to me like you're fighting a losing battle, Captain," she heard Paul Wooly say. "I know it's a cliché but there are other fish in the sea."

"But none with her kind of allure," Mike returned.

The husky edge in his voice caused a glow of delight and Emma felt herself weakening again. Maybe she was being too rigid. Maybe...

"Ahoy, Captain," a male voice called from the parking area. "Are you free for a night charter?"

"I'll need an hour to replenish my supplies," Mike called back.

Sharply Emma recalled the lonely nights her mother had spent while her father made his living. Her eyes turned to the sky. Right now it looked clear, but she'd heard the weatherman this morning say there was the possibility of an unexpected storm moving up the coast or blowing across from the gulf. It all depended on the strength and direction of the winds. An anxiousness for Mike suddenly swept through her. Her jaw firmed. That wasn't the kind of life she wanted to lead! Refusing to even look back, she climbed into her car and drove away.

Chapter Seven

Nearing her home, Emma saw a man sitting on the top step of her porch, his chin resting in his hands. It was Kenneth, still dressed in his golfing clothes. For a moment, she panicked. When he found out how she'd spent her day, would he be so angry with her that he'd decide to break off their relationship? Then she realized she didn't really care. With a sigh of regret, she admitted that she was having to try too hard to convince herself that she loved Kenneth. It was time to face the truth. She had no doubt he'd make someone a terrific husband but he wasn't her Mr. Right.

Mike Flint's image entered her mind. "And he isn't, either!" she snapped.

"Hi," Kenneth called out and rose as she parked.

"You look worried," she noted with concern, meeting him halfway to the house.

Turning and walking back to the porch with her, he

said bluntly, "Monica has come here to cause trouble. She told me she wants me back."

Anger and confusion showed on his face. But Emma also saw hurt in his eyes. "Are you so certain you don't want her back?"

"Absolutely not!"

They had reached the top step of the porch. Laying her hand on his arm, Emma stopped him. "We need to talk." She gave his arm a pull as she sat down on the step, letting him know she wanted him to join her.

Seating himself beside her, he took her hand in his. "You're the woman I want."

Emma faced him evenly. A part of her called her crazy for giving him up but another part knew she was doing the right thing for both of them. "If you didn't still have strong feelings for Monica, you wouldn't be so upset by her presence. I don't want to be the one you settle for because pride won't allow you to pick your first choice."

He scowled down at the step. "She didn't trust my feelings for her. She acted as if I were a gigolo."

"She told me her side of what happened between the two of you. I got the feeling she's matured a great deal. She knows she was mistaken and is now very certain of what she feels and what she wants."

Kenneth continued to glare at the step. "She told me that if I honestly had no feelings left for her, she would leave town tonight. I told her to go."

"If she honestly meant nothing to you, then you wouldn't be sitting here talking about her," Emma pointed out.

Releasing her hand, he raked his fingers through his hair. "I feel like a heel. You're perfect. You're everything I want in a wife. She can be headstrong and difficult."

"Has it ever occurred to you that you might find yourself getting bored with me?" Emma asked, then realized that down deep she'd begun to worry that she might get bored with him.

"We could have a very comfortable life together."

She cupped his face in her hands and gently forced him to look at her. "We are perfect for each other... almost. The problem is that the passion is missing. We're more like good friends than future lovers. When Monica is around, you can't seem to keep your attention off of her. She arouses your emotions in ways I never have. I think you should stop her from leaving town and give yourself some time to rethink your feelings."

"You're right," he conceded. When she released him, he kissed her on the tip of her nose. "I hope we will always be friends."

"We will," she assured him.

He smiled companionably, then rose and left.

Emma forced a smile as he drove off. Then resting her elbows on her knees and her chin in her hands, she allowed a frown to replace the smile as she stared unseeingly ahead and contemplated her future. She'd just sent Kenneth packing. Now what? Eventually her real Mr. Right would come along, she assured herself.

"Evening, darling." Her father's voice broke into her thoughts.

Blinking her eyes back into focus, she glanced over her shoulder to see him standing at the door.

"Kenneth was here. I invited him in but he said he'd rather wait outside. Did you see him?"

"I saw him." She eased herself to her feet.

Peter studied his daughter worriedly. "He looked like a man with something serious on his mind."

"It's another woman," she replied bluntly to his unasked question.

Fatherly pride caused anger to replace the worry. "I don't know how he could even look at another woman when he has you."

Emma smiled reassuringly. "It's all right, Dad. I knew there was something lacking in our relationship. I just didn't want to admit it. But I was already beginning to realize he wasn't the man for me."

Peter visibly relaxed. "I knew that. I just didn't figure it would do any good for me to say anything. You've always been headstrong and gone your own way." He winked his "knowing" wink at her. "But I could see that there was no gleam in your eyes when Kenneth entered a room. You were always glad to see him. I could tell that. But that added little sparkle that said he suddenly lit up the room was missing."

A reminiscent expression spread over his face. "And I know that look well. I'd see it on your mother's face when she'd see me and no matter what troubles I'd faced during the day, I felt like a hero."

Emma, too, recalled that loving look that seemed to actually add a glow to her mother's cheeks. "You," she said, giving her father a hug, "are an old romantic."

He looked hard into her face, the worry back in his eyes. "I'm just a man who wants his daughter to be happy."

"I am," she assured him.

"Well, you do look fine," he admitted with a nod of approval.

"How about some dinner?" she suggested.

Peter opened the door and waved her inside. "I've been working on a pot of my famous shrimp gumbo."

Passing him, Emma recalled that her father rarely cooked unless he was expecting company. The realization that he was probably intending to spend the evening viewing nautical charts with Mike Flint dawned on her. "If you're planning on Mike Flint joining us, forget it. He took out a night charter," she said over her shoulder.

"He called," her father replied, confirming her suspicion about her father's would-be plans for the evening. Peter caught up with her and placed an arm around her shoulders. "Looks like we're going to have a nice little father-daughter evening."

"Looks like." She found herself smiling at the prospect. Her father could be a trial, but he could also be enjoyable company and it had been a long time since they'd just sat and talked.

And we did have a lot of catching up to do, she mused awhile later as tears of laughter rolled down her cheeks. Her father had had a great many tales of antics that had occurred on the docks as well as descriptions of the idiosyncrasies of some of his charters he'd been saving up to tell her. The stories had taken them through dinner and dessert and now they were nearly finished cleaning the dishes. "I have missed our 'at home' evenings," she said, wiping her tears on the shoulder of her blouse as she handed him the last pan to dry.

"So have I," he replied.

Hating to see the evening end, she glanced toward the coffeepot. "There's some coffee left. How about if we go sit on the porch and finish it off."

He nodded. "Sounds like a fine idea."

A few minutes later as she curled up on the porch swing and he seated himself nearby in his rocking chair, he frowned up at the sky. "Clouds are gathering. That storm front the weatherman predicted was going to pass us by must have changed direction. Looks like we're in for a blow."

Emma noticed the wind had picked up and she could smell an added dampness in the air. Uninvitedly the thought of Mike out with his charter entered her mind. Her muscles tensed. He is not my concern, she snapped at herself.

"Emma?"

Her father's worried tones jerked her thoughts back to him.

"I was just asking if you recalled that trip to Savannah when you were ten?" he said, studying her narrowly. "But your mind must have been miles away. Are you sure you're all right about this breakup with Kenneth?"

"Honestly, I'm fine," she replied. "I was just hoping that any night charters are keeping an eye on the weather." She nearly gasped when she realized she'd actually spoken aloud what was on her mind. At least I spoke in generalities, she fumed at herself. The last thing she wanted was for her father to guess Mike Flint had caused her even a moment's anxiety.

Peter nodded knowingly. "We've got a pretty savvy lot. Reckon most will be putting into port before long."

"You're right," Emma agreed. Then determined to keep her mind off of the weather, she added, "And I do remember that trip to Savannah. It was the one where you bought Mom that painted fan she loved so much."

Peter smiled reminiscently. "Yes, the fan."

He grew silent and Emma knew he was again thinking of her mother. There was a gentleness on his face that told her his thoughts were of the good times. Feeling as if speaking would be intruding, she remained silent.

"It's getting late. I think I'll go to bed and read awhile," he announced a few minutes later, easing himself out of his chair.

Emma's attention had again been drawn to the clouds gathering and now periodically masking the moon. Turning back to her father, she noticed the shadow of melancholy in his eyes. Rising, she gave him a hug. "I love you, Daddy," she said. "And I miss her, too."

He smiled down at her. "My greatest hope is that you will find someone who will bring you the same happiness your mother brought me."

"I'm trying," she replied.

He gave an encouraging nod, then went inside.

Emma had started to follow when she heard the first raindrop hit. It was so large, it splatted. Immediately it was followed by more. The night turned black as the rain came hard and fast. The wind whipped around and she was forced inside to keep from getting wet.

Standing at the window looking out, the image of the *Reliable Lady* being tossed on raging waves filled her mind. The storm had moved in even faster than she'd expected. It was possible he wouldn't have had time to get back to port. Panic swept through her. A cold sweat broke out on the palms of her hands. "Nights like this are a perfect example of why I have no intention of falling in love with a seaman," she hissed under her breath.

Again she told herself that Mike Flint was not her concern. Determined to put him out of her mind, she turned away from the window with the intention of doing as her father had . . . go to bed and curl up with a good book. But halfway up the stairs, she came to a halt. "I have an errand I have to run," she called up to her dad.

"It's raining cats and dogs out there." She heard his yelled protest from the upstairs landing as she strode to the back door.

"I won't be gone long," she called back over her shoulder, her tone letting him know arguing would be useless.

"Drive safely," he growled, and mentally she could see him shaking his head as if he thought she was nuts.

"And I am," she muttered under her breath, pulling on her slicker, then making a dash for her car.

The rain hit her windshield like a sheet of water making it impossible at times for the wipers to provide her with clear vision. To her relief there was almost no other traffic on the roads. "Everyone else was smart enough to stay at home," she fumed at herself as she drove toward the marina. "I cannot believe I'm doing this!" Still, she continued.

To her relief the rain began to slacken. By the time she reached the parking area, it had calmed considerably. Pulling up to where she could see the *Reliable Lady*'s slip from her car, she peered out. The boat was there. While she watched, a lone figure came out of the cabin. He was dressed in a mackintosh with the hood pulled over his head, but she knew without a doubt it was Mike. As if he sensed someone watching him, he turned in her direction.

Quickly she shifted into gear and drove away. The last thing she wanted was to encourage him by letting him guess she'd been concerned. Self-directed anger raged through her. If she hadn't known he was out, then she could have been home, all comfortable and cozy, and not out in this weather. "And I was only so worried because I've known him all my life and would not want anything bad to happen to him," she told herself. "However, in the future, I will make it a point to avoid learning anything about his activities. His business is his business and not mine," she finished firmly.

Peter Wynn was waiting in the kitchen for his daughter when she returned. "Did you get your errand run?" he asked.

"Yes," she said through the back screen door as she hung her slicker on a hook on the back porch.

"Must have been pretty important," he persisted when she entered.

"It was just one of those needling little nuisances that prey on your mind until they're taken care of," she replied, refusing to divulge any details of her expedition.

"But it's taken care of now and you're not planning to go out again?" he asked.

She'd slipped off her shoes and set them aside to dry. Now she straightened and faced him. "I've taken care of it and have no intention of allowing it to plague me further."

For a long moment, he regarded her in silence, then he said with fatherly concern, "I know it's hard for you not to have a mother to talk to, but I'm a pretty good listener. If you've got a problem you want to discuss, I'm here."

"Honestly, I have no problem that needs discussing," she assured him.

"Well, you do look as if you mean what you're saying," he conceded.

"Of course I do," she returned with an even stronger note of assurance in her voice. Then giving him a hug, she bid him good-night and went up to her room.

"Michael Flint is not a problem. He's not even a nuisance," she reaffirmed under her breath a little later as she crawled into bed. Still, when she closed her eyes, the image of the man in the mackintosh on the deck of his vessel filled her mind.

"Go away!" she growled, and forced the image out.

The next morning as she applied a little extra makeup to hide the lingering traces of a restless night, Emma silently cursed Mike Flint. He'd meandered uninvited through her dreams. And ever since she'd woken this morning, she'd had the most peculiar feeling that he was nearby. "Forget about him," she again ordered herself and finished dressing for church.

She knew her father had a charter that morning and wouldn't be going with her. But then he'd never been much of a churchgoer, anyway. He always claimed he did his best conversing with God when he was out on the open sea.

Descending the stairs, she heard him in the kitchen. "Morni..." The greeting she'd been issuing upon joining him died on her lips. Her father was by the back door pulling on his windbreaker in preparation for leaving while seated comfortably at the table as if he planned on staying awhile was Mike Flint. That she'd been aware of his presence before she'd even come downstairs shook her. I wasn't really *aware* he was here. He'd simply been on her mind from last night and that had caused her to feel as if he was close by, she reasoned. His actual being there was merely coincidence.

Recovering from her shock, she saw that he was dressed for church in slacks, a white shirt and tie and she found herself thinking that he did look handsome. Immediately she shoved that thought from her mind.

Peter regarded his daughter with interest. "Mike's been telling me you crewed for him yesterday."

"I did," she responded to the question in his voice. "I went down to the pier hoping to go out with you but you'd already left and Captain Flint needed another hand."

"You taught her well, Peter," Mike spoke up. "She knows her way around a boat."

Peter's gaze narrowed on his daughter. "Whether she likes admitting it or not, she's got a bit of my sea-water in her blood."

Emma met his gaze levelly. "I've no problem with admitting to having a little seawater in my blood. I simply don't want to be married to it."

Peter sighed, then an expression of fatherly understanding spread over his face. "We've all got to follow our own star." He suddenly grinned. "And my daughter is one who, once she's determined what she wants, not even a team of tugboats can pull her off course."

"Sometimes currents can take an unexpected turn and even the most sturdy craft gets swept along," Mike noted.

Emma could feel his gaze on her even before she turned to him. "This helmsman knows how to steer her craft away from dangerous waters."

A gleam of pleasure sparked in Mike's eyes. "So you admit there is a danger that if you let yourself get too close, you could be swept away."

Emma scowled at him. "I know my course and I have no intention of being swept off of it."

"Well, well, well," Peter Wynn mused while, inwardly, Emma cringed at the knowing tone in her father's voice. "Seems there's a bit more going on between the two of you than I'd realized." His grin broadened. Approaching the table, he extended his hand to Mike. "Good luck, you'll need it." He glanced toward Emma. "You could do worse." Then with a chuckle, he waved goodbye and left.

Emma groaned. "He'd better not try any matchmaking," she muttered threateningly.

"That sounds like a woman who's afraid she might weaken."

Emma turned to glare at the man seated at her kitchen table. "I will not."

Challenge flicked in his eyes. "I could have sworn I saw you at the marina last night. Could it be that you were worried enough about me, you came to make sure I got in all right?"

"I just felt the need to take a drive," she lied.

He cocked an eyebrow in disbelief. "In the middle of a storm?"

Her jaw firmed. "Yes, in the middle of a storm."

For a moment, he looked as if he was going to continue to argue this point, then his expression relaxed and he said, "Can I give you a lift to church or is Kenneth coming by to pick you up?"

Obviously her father had not told him about her breakup with Kenneth. Well, she wasn't going to mention it. Besides, it was none of his business. "I have a ride to church."

He nodded as if that was what he'd expected and rose from the table. Picking up an envelope that was lying beside his coffee cup, he extended it to her. "Your wages from yesterday. You took off so fast, I didn't get a chance to give them to you."

"Thanks," she replied, careful to accept the envelope without touching his hand.

Reaching across the table, he traced the line of her jaw with the tips of his fingers. "Just in case you were there last night because you were worried about me, thanks for the concern. I liked the idea of having someone waiting for me to return."

As she'd been afraid it would, his touch sent warm currents surging through her. Shakily she admitted that the physical attraction she felt for him was strong.

Then she recalled the panic she'd experienced when the storm had built so suddenly. This was one attraction she would not give in to. She took a step back breaking the contact. "I'm sure there are several unattached women in town who would happily await your return." Something that felt like a jab of jealousy pierced her. Determinedly she ignored it.

He frowned impatiently. "Through the years I have looked around. But like a magnet drawn to due north, my mind keeps coming back to you. And I'd wager you've thought about me every once in a while." An expression that dared her to deny this spread over his face. "Last winter when I had the flu, you were the one person who showed up on my doorstep. And with your own homemade chicken soup, no less."

Her back stiffened defensively. "I knew you were alone and that flu was dangerous. I thought someone should check on you to make certain you weren't so ill you couldn't take care of yourself." Not wanting him to guess she'd lost a night's sleep worrying about him before she'd finally gone by to check on him, she added with forced nonchalance, "I would have sent my father but I was afraid he might catch the bug and he's worse than any child when he's sick."

Rounding the table, he approached her and cupped her face in his hands. Challenge again flashed in his eyes as his gaze bore into her. "Through the years, I'd swear I've seen you looking my way more than once."

For a moment all she could think about was the exciting feel of his work-callused palms against her skin. Then she saw his face coming closer to hers and knew he intended to kiss her. Terrified her body would betray her, she jerked free and backed away. "I might have looked but I have no intention of touching," she said shakily.

Her confession caused the blue of his eyes to darken with triumph. "We belong together, Emma. You know that."

"No, I don't know that. What I know is that I find you attractive. But I also find Robert Redford and Mel Gibson attractive. It's merely a physical thing."

His gaze narrowed and he took a step toward her. When she took a step back, he stopped and the impatient frown returned to his face. "There is nothing 'mere' about the 'physical thing' I feel for you and the look I see in your eyes suggests that whatever you're feeling is strong enough to come close to sending you into a panic."

Emma's defenses were dangerously weakening. Again she reminded herself of the fear that had caused her to drive to the marina in spite of the raging storm. "I will not spend my life pacing the floor, waiting for the sea to send my man back to me," she said in a low growl.

His frown darkened. "You are the most single-minded woman I've ever known. Be careful you don't let that stubborn streak of yours cause you to settle for less than what you truly want in life," he cautioned. Heading for the door, he added over his shoulder, "I'll be seeing you."

Momentarily his warning threatened her resolve, then her shoulders squared. "Not if I see you first," she muttered under her breath as the door closed behind him.

* * *

Church, Emma confessed silently a few hours later, had been mildly uncomfortable. It was early afternoon now. She was dressed in shorts and, drowsy from the afternoon heat, sat propped up by pillows on the porch swing.

Frowning, she recalled her entrance into the sanctuary. When she'd walked in alone, several people had glanced her way and she'd seen more than mere greetings on their faces. She guessed that Kenneth had taken Monica out to dinner last night and rumors were already flying.

However, she was fairly certain those who noted her entrance didn't know for sure she and Kenneth had broken up. There had been more of a questioning look in their eyes than the usual sympathetic one reserved for the person perceived to be the jilted party. And she had no doubt that once people did learn of the breakup she would be cast in that role. After all, Kenneth was the one with the new love interest.

Then there had been Mike. From the moment she'd stepped through the door, she'd been aware of his presence. Furious with herself for not being able to put him out of her mind, she'd again ordered herself to ignore him.

Hoping to quell any rumors about her suffering from a broken heart before they even got started, she smiled brightly and nodded a good-morning to those who looked her way as she continued down the aisle and slipped into her usual pew.

Martha Balanski normally sat toward the middle of the pew. Today, she scooted over until she was right beside Emma. "Kenneth's not here with you?" she asked in a low whisper.

"No," Emma replied, offering no further explanation. Now, she had decided, wasn't the time to go into any details.

"Susan Marley said she saw Kenneth and that red-headed woman having dinner together," Martha persisted. Her manner became motherly protective. "He's not two-timing you, is he?"

"No." Knowing that she was going to have to say something, Emma added, "We realized that we were very fond of each other but as friends, nothing more."

Martha patted her hand in a comforting fashion. "You'll find someone even better."

Seeing the continued concern in Martha's eyes, Emma gave her a reassuring smile. "I know I will. Honestly, I'm not upset about this. I know it was the right thing to do."

Martha breathed a sigh of relief. "I'm so glad." Abruptly she smiled and waved at someone beyond Emma's shoulder. "That handsome Mike Flint is looking our way. Now he's a man I've always considered an excellent catch. And he does seem to find you attractive."

Emma knew Martha was recalling the kiss in front of the bookstore. Against her will, a thread of delight wove through her as she remembered the feel of his lips on hers. "Then you're welcome to him," she replied, again refusing to give in to these traitorous emotions.

Martha shook her head as if to say she really didn't understand Emma's attitude and turned her attention to finding the first hymn they would be singing from the hymnal.

Following the service, Emma had stayed around long enough to exchange a few greetings and appear relaxed and at ease with the world.

Now, as she stretched and picked up the glass of lemonade from a nearby table and took a sip, she hoped her behavior along with Martha spreading the word that the breakup was a mutually friendly affair would put a stop to any rumors of her being jilted.

"Hi," a familiar female voice broke into Emma's thoughts.

Emma had again closed her eyes. She opened them to see Katie approaching.

"I was out for a walk and decided I should come by to see if you were really all right," Katie said bluntly, seating herself in a nearby rocker.

Emma read the deep concern on her friend's face. "I'm fine, really," she replied. "Kenneth and I simply admitted that, although we are very fond of each other, the passion was missing. We parted friends and I wish him the very best and vice versa."

Katie visibly relaxed. "I'm glad to hear that." A haunted look suddenly shadowed her eyes. "It's not right for someone to walk away without any explanation and barely a word of goodbye."

Emma had the strongest feeling they weren't talking about her anymore. But before she could think of a subtle way to probe, Katie abruptly rose.

"I've got to get going. There's some painting I want to do this afternoon. Seems that old house of mine is always in need of repairing or mending these days," she said, and with a final goodbye, she left.

Watching the slender brown-haired woman walking away, Emma couldn't forget the haunted look she'd seen in Katie's eyes. A man had once deeply hurt her friend. Of that she was sure.

"Some men are trouble with a capital *T*," she mused. Mike Flint's image immediately came into her mind. "But I've always been smart enough not to play with fire and I don't intend to start now."

Leaning back and closing her eyes once again, she frowned thoughtfully. Maybe she'd been going about finding her Mr. Right the wrong way. So far, she'd simply bided her time waiting for him to come along. Maybe she should do some active searching. There was the new history teacher at the high school. He'd come into the store several times and he'd made a point of speaking to her.

He was pleasant and nice looking. But he'd bored her. "However, he could be like the dress that looks terrible on the hanger but when you try it on, it's magnificent," she mused.

Again Mike Flint's face filled her mind. "No!" she growled. Furious that she couldn't even relax without the man creeping into her thoughts, she pushed herself off the swing. A brisk walk was what she needed, she decided. But as she started inside to get her keys so she could lock the house, a car pulling up in front caught her attention.

Chapter Eight

Turning to see who had arrived, Emma inwardly cringed. Clearly the rumormongers were painting her as the injured party. She was pretty sure there wasn't a female in town who wouldn't have recognized that red Porsche. It belonged to Lance Pitney, the town Casanova and self-appointed soother of broken hearts.

"Afternoon," the tall, handsome, black-haired owner of the red sports car called out in a friendly drawl as he strode toward the house. "Thought you might like a shoulder to lean on."

Emma smiled. At least the man was blunt. "No, but thanks," she replied.

He looked mildly confused. "I heard you and Drake broke up. He went chasing after a redhead from his past."

"We did and he is, but I'm fine. We parted

friends," she replied, feeling like a broken record.

"Too bad." Exaggerated disappointment showed on his face. "I had a lovely afternoon planned. I thought we'd go on a picnic."

Emma found herself smiling. Lance did have charm. He made her feel pretty and very wanted. But she did not need the attention of a fortuitous lecher to bolster her ego. "I..." she began, intending to send him on his way when the screeching of a vehicle coming much too quickly to a stop interrupted. Looking to the street she saw Mike's blue pickup parked behind the sports car.

In the next instant, he was out of the cab. Shoving the door closed with a loud bang, he strode up the walk. "She doesn't need your kind of help," he growled at Lance as he reached the man.

Emma was sure that beneath his perfect tan, Lance actually paled. "Seems you've already got a shoulder to lean on," he said, and without any further word of goodbye, he turned and walked back to his car.

Mike scowled at the man's departing back. "I figured that barracuda would show up pretty quick." He swung his attention to Emma. "I won't say I'm sorry you and Drake have broken up, but I was hoping the break would be because you'd finally admitted that you care about me, not because he'd discovered a preference for redheads." A gruffness entered his voice. "Are you all right?"

Emma could not deny the honest concern she saw on his face. "I'm fine," she replied firmly.

For a long moment, he studied her narrowly as if uncertain as to whether to believe her not, then said, "Paul took the *Reliable Lady* on a charter today. I've got a salvage job this afternoon up one of the tributaries... a small cabin cruiser, twenty feet. The kind that sleeps two cozily if they're not claustrophobic. Some woman wanted to redecorate her house but her husband refused to give her the money. They got into an argument about how much he was spending on his boat. The argument ended when she walked down to their private dock and put a couple of shotgun blasts through the hull. The boat sank like a rock. If the current picks it up, it'll become a hazard to other river traffic. Besides, he wants it brought up and repaired." His jaw formed a hard line. "And you're coming with me. Pitney isn't the only cruiser in this town who might try to take advantage of you."

Refusal formed on the tip of her tongue. But before a word could issue, she stopped herself. Ignoring him hadn't worked. No matter how hard she tried, she could not keep him from constantly popping into her mind. Maybe a change of strategy was the key to getting him out of her system. Besides, the thought of sitting around her house all day caused an unbearable restlessness. "Sure, why not," she said with an indifferent air. "Just give me a chance to get my keys."

Surprise registered on his face. "I figured I'd practically have to drag you kicking and screaming."

She smiled dryly at his obvious shock and, for the first time, felt as if she had the upper hand. "If I stay here, friends will probably drop by to console me and I don't feel like spending the entire day trying to convince people I don't need consoling. I figure any port in a storm will do."

His expression became shuttered as he nodded acceptance of this explanation.

But while she wrote her father a quick note to let him know where she was going, then gathered the things she thought she'd need for a day on the water, Emma became more and more aware of his continued silence. By the time she was seated in the cab of his truck, her nerves were taut. When he climbed in behind the wheel she noted his expression had grown grim. "Look, if you've decided you don't want me to come along, just say so," she demanded curtly, thinking she might have already found her cure.

"I want you with me now and for always," he growled. "But I don't want you on the rebound."

He thought she was pining over Kenneth! Impatience flashed in her eyes. "I am *not* on the rebound."

"Then why this sudden change of heart?" he challenged, disbelief clear in his voice and on his face. "Until this afternoon, you've been trying to avoid me like I had the plague."

She glared at him. "I most definitely have not had a *change of heart*. I'm merely changing my tactics." She bit back a gasp at her bluntness. She'd meant to keep the real reason for accompanying him to herself.

He cocked an eyebrow questioningly.

A self-conscious flush began to creep up her neck. Well, she had always preferred the truth to pretense, she reminded herself and her shoulders squared. "As I already admitted earlier today, I do find you physically attractive. It has occurred to me that maybe I've made you seem more attractive to myself by declaring you off-limits," she elaborated coolly.

For a long moment he studied her in silence. Then he shook his head as if he found her logic bewildering. "That is an interesting theory. I'd never have thought of it. You've convinced me that trying to understand the female mind is a waste of time." Shifting the car into gear, he pulled out onto the street.

Emma knew he owned a couple of acres of waterfront land where he housed his salvage vessels but she'd never seen it. The site was a few miles out of town on one of the tributaries. She expected the land surrounding the dock to be mostly unkempt. Instead, they turned onto a paved driveway. To her left a plot had been cleared and an attractively carved wooden sign with Flint Enterprises highlighted in blue paint across the front stood among a bed of flowers. As they approached the dock, more land had been cleared. There was a large paved parking lot from which a concrete path led to a small brick, single-story building. A second professionally carved wooden sign erected along the walkway designated the building as the offices of Flint Enterprises. On both sides of the walkway were flower beds and another small bed surrounded the base of the sign.

"This place is much nicer than I expected," she admitted as Mike parked his truck alongside an old Jeep, a yellow pickup truck and blue Mustang already there.

"I've been fixing it up," he replied in response to the surprise in her voice. "There's a deep enough channel running into here that I could operate my charter service from here. But so far, I've kept that part of my business at the marina. Customers can find that location more easily and many of them feel more comfortable with an in-town address. Also, a lot of people like to come down and take a look at the boats before they choose one."

Emma had never really taken a close look at the businessman side of Mike Flint before. He was calm, cool and thoughtful. Amazement swept through her as she realized how powerful a sense of confidence in his abilities he inspired within her.

His gaze had shifted to the dock and his jaw set with purpose. "However, through the years, I've built up a steady clientele and they've sent me new customers. I'm seriously considering increasing my docking space and moving my entire business out here fairly soon."

"I'm sure you could make a success of it," she heard herself saying, thinking that if any man could accomplish his goals in life, that man would be Mike Flint. With the exception of breaking my resolve, she stipulated.

He grinned at her and a sudden heat showed in his eyes. "I've just purchased the adjoining five acres. I'm thinking about building a house on it." As he spoke, he eased a strand of hair back behind her ear.

When he trailed his finger along the curve of the lobe, then into the hollow behind her ear, she had to fight to keep from gasping with pleasure.

"Figured I'd let you choose the floor plan."

The temptation to agree to almost anything he said was strong. You came here to fight this weakness, she reminded herself. She took a step back, breaking the contact. "And what if your future wife doesn't like my choice?" she asked, marveling at the fact that she'd actually sounded calm and coherent.

For a moment renewed impatience showed on his face, then his expression became shuttered and he motioned toward the pier. "Looks like Sam, Garth and Pete have the rigs ready to go."

She turned to see Sam Henley waving to them. Emma had known Sam all of her life. He was in his thirties, married with three children and, like Mike and her father, had a boat he chartered. When he didn't have a charter, he fished and occasionally worked for Mike.

Garth Smith was also a local. At barely twenty years of age, he was considered one of the best divers around. His dad owned one of the hardware stores in town and Garth worked for him. But whenever he had a chance, he took on diving jobs.

Pete Delany was in his late sixties. He was officially retired, but he still spent his days hanging around the docks and crewing on any ship where an extra hand was needed. Emma was sure Mike had hired him for this job because it was well-known that Pete knew these inland waterways like the back of his hand.

She waved back as she and Mike headed to the pier. Nearing the pusher, she had to admit to a sense of excitement. This strong, heavy vessel that resembled a tugboat except for its flattened prow, which allowed it to push the barge, had always fascinated her. Then her gaze shifted with interest to the barge with the attached crane that would be used to hoist the sunken cruiser out of the water. This was definitely a much more interesting way of spending the day than sitting on her porch trying to convince well-wishers that they had no reason to pity her, she decided.

"You look like a kid eyeing a new toy."

Emma glanced at Mike to find him regarding her with a pleased expression on his face. "I always enjoy an opportunity to learn new things," she replied honestly.

"I'll be happy to teach you anything you'd like to learn," he volunteered.

Again the blue of his eyes darkened with a heat that tempted her. "I'll keep that in mind," she heard herself saying. That response had actually sounded flirtatious! she berated herself. The last thing she wanted to do was encourage him.

He grinned and winked and, in spite of the anger she'd just directed at herself, her toes curled with delight. This isn't working out the way I planned, she wailed silently. The thought that she should simply turn and run as fast as she could in the other direction flashed through her mind. But that would be cowardly and it wouldn't solve anything, she countered as she climbed aboard the pusher.

"This was the dumbest thing I've ever done," the short, slender, gray-haired woman who had introduced herself as Brenda Oates muttered grumpily.

With Pete at the helm of the pusher prepared to act if either boat broke their moorings and Sam concentrating on the crane, Emma had determined that it would be best if she simply stayed out of the men's way. Unable to shake a nagging anxiousness for Mike, she'd taken the small dinghy from the pusher and rowed to the pier where the sunken boat had been moored. Now she was standing above the spot where it had gone down. Below the surface of the water, Mike and Garth were working harnesses around the vessel.

In her teens, she'd done quite a bit of scuba diving and knew there were always risks. And those risks were even higher in these waters. There was more debris. To make matters worse, getting the harness strapped around the sunken boat was stirring up mud and sand from the river bottom making the visibility extremely limited. Her nerves grew more taut as she worried about the vessel shifting and trapping one of them. Trying not to think of the dangers, she turned to the woman who had spoken.

"He just made me so angry," Brenda continued. "All I wanted was to redecorate the house." She scowled down at the water. "Daniel hardly ever even took that stupid boat out. Most of the time it just stayed moored here at the dock. But he made sure it was constantly maintained, ready to go at a moment's whim. And every evening he'd come down here after supper and sit on the deck and smoke a cigar."

Brenda paused to scowl around Emma at the plump, balding man gazing down at the water. "Now he sits in the den or on the patio after supper and smokes. I've always hated the smell of cigars. I can't wait until he has his damn boat back!"

"A man needs his own private thinking place." Daniel Oates spoke up in his defense, taking his eyes off the murky waters to meet his wife's hostile gaze.

Brenda rewarded her husband's comment with a *humph* and stalked off the pier and up to the house.

Daniel watched his wife's departing back until the back door had slammed behind her, then he turned to Emma. "I should have told her to go ahead and redecorate. It's just that I like the house the way it is. My chair in the den fits me just right and I know that's the first thing she'll want to get rid of. She's been claiming for the past five years that the thing's an eyesore." He shook his head sadly. "'Course I never thought she'd get so crazy she'd shoot my boat."

"Life can be unpredictable," Emma agreed, knowing that if someone had told her this morning that she'd be spending the afternoon watching the bubbles from scuba tanks rising to the surface and feeling frantic for even a glimpse of the men working beneath, she wouldn't have believed them. A headache began to build as she returned her attention to the water.

This strain on her nerves was exactly why she'd steered a course away from Mike Flint. And this afternoon's experience will most certainly be a cure for the attraction she'd been feeling toward him, she assured herself.

Two heads suddenly bobbed up out of the water and relief swept through her. But it was short-lived. Mike waved to the barge and Sam began to maneuver the crane, lowering its cable so that the divers could get hold of the huge hook on the end. Emma felt dizzy and realized she'd been holding her breath while praying the hook wouldn't accidentally hit either of the men in the water. A part of her was tempted to walk off the pier and never look back, but a stronger part made her stay. If there was trouble, she wanted to be there, ready to jump in and help.

"Those two sure know their business," Daniel remarked with admiration when the final sling was attached to the cable.

"Yes," she replied, again experiencing a rush of relief.

As Garth swam to the barge, Mike turned to Emma and the man on the pier. "It'd be best if you two moved onto dry land, just in case the boat swings in your direction,'' he ordered.

Emma was aware that he watched them until he was sure they were out of danger before he swam to the barge to join Garth and Sam. As the three men worked to carefully bring the boat out of the water and secure it to the barge, she had to admit that Mike took no chances. He was careful and precise in his work. And the work he did was important to the safety of the waterways and those who used them, she added, then mentally groaned. She was supposed to be working on lessening her feelings for the man, not building up an admiration for him.

''I've got to be getting back to the pusher,'' she announced abruptly when Mike jumped back into the water and swam for shore. She knew he was coming to reconfirm with the boat's owner the destination to which he'd be taking the damaged vessel. A part of her suggested that the polite thing to do would be to wait and offer him a ride back, but for the moment, she wanted to keep a distance between them.

She'd secured the dinghy and was standing on the deck of the pusher watching Sam make a final inspection of the straps they'd put on the retrieved vessel when Mike joined her.

''Now all we have to do is deliver the boat to dry dock and we're done,'' he said with satisfaction.

He and Garth had both been wearing full body suits over their swimming trunks as added protection against debris, unfriendly creatures or being scraped by the vessel they were rescuing. As he pushed the hood off and ran his fingers through his damp, matted hair, freeing it to be dried by the breeze, Emma had the most tremendous urge to run her own fingers through the thick, blond strands.

Then he began to unzip the heavy rubber suit and her blood seemed to actually heat. Unable to stop herself, she watched him shedding the protective covering. The definition of the muscles in his arms and shoulders enticed her to touch them to test their strength. Shaken by the intensity of this desire, she silently ordered herself to behave and took a step back.

The retreat, however, only served to provide her with a better view of him working his way further out of the garment. His hard flat abdomen sent a heated thrill of delight racing through her. As her gaze moved admiringly downward toward the strong, sturdy columns of his legs and then along them, her blood raced. You're being absolutely wanton, she chided herself. Still she could not stop from slowly trailing her gaze upward for a second complete look.

"If you don't stop looking at me that way, I may not be responsible for my actions," he warned gruffly.

Meeting his gaze, Emma forced an expression of innocence. "I'm sure I don't know what you mean."

He cocked an eyebrow in disbelief. "You were leering."

A red flush of embarrassment began building from her neck upward. He'd called her bluff and her body had betrayed her. "Men are always making inspections of women," she returned with schooled nonchalance. "A little turnabout is only fair play."

"Can I assume you found everything satisfactory?"

There was amusement in his eyes but behind the jesting mask, Emma was certain she saw a hint of anxiousness. The male ego peeking through, she thought dryly. "Satisfactory," she conceded.

An impish mischievousness spread over his features. "Maybe a little more than satisfactory?" he coaxed.

She couldn't stop herself grinning back. "I don't have a lot of experience to make comparisons from."

The blue of his eyes darkened with purpose. "And I intend to convince you to keep it that way."

The thought that he could convince her of just about anything crossed her mind. Without even realizing what she was doing, she took a step toward him. His smile deepened to one of triumph as she took a second step in his direction.

"Hey, boss, you ready to get moving to the dry dock?"

Emma jerked around at the sound of Sam's voice. She drew a shaky breath as she realized how close she'd come to literally throwing herself into Mike's arms. Turning back to him, she saw a flash of impatient anger directed over her shoulder in Sam's direction. Then he breathed a resigned sigh. "We'll finish this discussion later," he said, dropping a light kiss on the tip of her nose as if sealing a promise.

Before she could tell him that she had no intention of "finishing" this conversation, he'd gone to join the other men. Today is definitely not working out the way I planned, she moaned quietly, her gaze falling on his discarded scuba suit and the memory of him stripping it off causing a renewed heat to spread through her.

She shifted her attention to the house beyond the dock. The gray-haired woman was standing on the porch, arms akimbo, watching them. It would seem that both she and I have learned the hard way that acting on an impulse can get you more than you bargained for, Emma mused.

"I hope your silence is because you're relaxed and enjoying yourself and not because you're bored." Mike's voice broke the stillness that had been filling the cab of his truck for the past several minutes.

Ever since they'd finished with the salvage job, bid goodbye to Sam, Garth and Pete and driven away from Mike's place of business, Emma had been purposefully staring out the window, attempting not to think about the man behind the wheel. But darkness had fallen and as they drove through the shadowy night, she seemed to be even more aware of his presence. Giving up trying not to look at him, she turned to him. "I'm just tired. It's been a long day," she replied.

Finding herself wanting to trace the line of his jaw with her fingertip, she breathed a frustrated sigh, leaned back and closed her eyes.

The truck slowed, then stopped and she guessed they were at a red light. Opening her eyes once again, she saw that Mike was frowning.

"You don't have to be polite with me, just honest," he growled. "I know today wasn't like the fancy afternoons you spent at the country club. But I wasn't going to leave you to a wolf like Pitney."

Realizing he'd mistaken the cause of her sigh, she considered letting his anger remain between them. It made a safe barrier. But instead, she heard herself saying, "I wasn't being politely evasive. I did find this afternoon interesting." Her gaze shifted to the front window. "I used to get terribly bored on those long afternoons playing golf or sitting around trying to make small talk. I don't think I'm cut out to be one of the country club set."

Mentally she gasped when she realized how open she'd been. She'd meant to stop with merely assuring him she hadn't been bored. Instead she'd revealed thoughts, that until now, had been locked away in her mind ... thoughts she'd tried to bury in order to convince herself that she and Kenneth could have a good life together.

He visibly relaxed but his frown remained as he said with gruff apology, "I also hope you don't mind missing the gourmet meals I'm sure you ate with Kenneth. It's late and I'm too tired to take you home, go home and clean up, and pick you up for a very late dinner. How does pizza sound to you?"

The remembered mingled aromas of cheese, pepperoni, tomato sauce and bread caused her mouth to water. "It's one of my favorite foods."

This time his frown vanished completely. A block later, he turned into the parking lot of a favorite local pizzeria. But as he turned off the engine and Emma started to climb out of the cab, he caught her by the wrist, stopping her exit.

The heat of his touch caused her to momentarily forget her hunger. She turned to him questioningly, wondering if he was going to kiss her.

He studied her narrowly as if trying to read her thoughts. "Is this day going as well as I think it is?"

"Let's just say it isn't going the way I planned," she replied stiffly.

"I'm very glad to hear that," he said, his mouth moving toward hers.

Don't go so fast, she warned herself, still hoping his effect on her was only going to be temporary. Still, she could not make herself even attempt to evade the kiss. A silence, made intense by expectation, surrounded them as she waited for his lips to meet hers.

Suddenly the stillness was broken by a long, low grumble. Realizing it was her stomach, Emma blushed.

With a chuckle, Mike abruptly straightened away from her. "I think I should get you fed immediately."

Disappointment at having missed being kissed by him was so strong she had to swallow a groan of frustration. "Yes, food," she muttered, grabbing for the handle of the door. Climbing down from the cab, she couldn't believe how much she'd wanted him to kiss her. Or how natural his hand on her shoulder felt as he guided her to the door of the eatery.

Even more disconcerting was the way her legs weakened when his hand moved slowly to the small of her back as they entered. The urge to turn right then and there and kiss him was so intense it took all of her control to stop herself.

Had this been why she'd steered such a wide path around him all these years? she wondered, slipping into a booth by a window. Had her instincts known she wouldn't be able to resist him if she got too close? As if in answer, he slid into the booth next to her and his leg brushed hers. Deep within, a fire like none she'd ever experienced before blazed to life. Then his leg settled against hers and her whole body felt as if it had gone up in flames.

Nothing this strong can be real, she reasoned frantically. She was simply in a weakened state because she was so tired and hungry.

Realizing the palms of her hands were damp, she started to dry them on the legs of her shorts before picking up her menu. Big mistake! she growled at herself as the side of her hand brushed against Mike's denim encased thigh and the sturdy feel of him caused her breath to lock in her lungs.

"I think it'd be safer if I sat across the table," he said huskily, slipping quickly off their shared bench and onto the one opposite her.

She looked up to see a passion that matched her own reflected in the blue depths of his eyes. "This can't be happening," she muttered, and jerked her attention to her menu.

Mike slipped a finger under her chin and forced her to look at him once again. "My grandfather always told me that a man's survival depends on trusting his instincts."

"Right now, I wouldn't trust mine to get me safely across a street," she replied.

His expression became solemn. "I promise you, I'll always do everything in my power to protect you from harm."

Her jaw tensed. "It's not me I'd spend my life worrying about if I let this go any further."

He traced the line of her jaw, sending currents of excitement trailing through her. Again her body betrayed her. Her cheeks flushed with pleasure at his touch and she saw the blue of his eyes deepen with satisfaction. "Are you really willing to settle for something less than what we could have together?" he asked.

For as long as she could remember, she'd known what she didn't want . . . a man who was bound to the sea. Now she felt only confusion. Seeing the waitress approaching, she saw her escape and took it. "Right now I'd settle for a pizza with everything on it," she said.

Mike cocked an eyebrow at her evasive maneuver. Then he grinned dryly. "I've always known that beneath that cool, controlled exterior beats the heart of a woman who wants all that life can offer."

Again the desire to accept all that Mike Flint could offer was strong. Then she remembered the long, anxious afternoon she'd spent watching him work. She wanted a peaceful life and she'd never have that married to him. Jerking her gaze away from him, she smiled a greeting at the waitress who had arrived.

When the woman left a few minutes later with their order, Emma's jaw firmed. She knew she was in danger of allowing her confusion to cause her to admit more than she wanted to if Mike continued their discussion from where they had been interrupted. "My father thinks the weather will hold for the rest of the week," she said.

Again he regarded her dryly, letting her know he saw through her ploy to turn the conversation to neutral waters. And for a moment she was sure he was going to challenge her. Then, as if he'd used up the last of his energy, the tiredness caused by the heavy work he'd done that day suddenly spread across his face. "Looks like it to me, too," he said, the last word garbled by a yawn.

She frowned at him worriedly. "You look exhausted. You should have dropped me off and gone straight home."

He shrugged. "I needed to eat." Leaning his elbows on the table, he propped his head in his hands facing her. "Read any good books lately?"

She knew what he was doing. He was too tired to even think so he was turning the conversation over to her. "Why don't you lean back and take a short nap," she suggested. "I'll wake you when the pizza arrives."

He looked as if he was going to protest, then he straightened and eased his shoulders back into the corner of the booth. "I'm sorry," he apologized. "It's not the company," he added as he closed his eyes and quickly drifted off to sleep.

Emma tried to feel insulted but she couldn't. What was even worse was that she discovered she was actually deriving pleasure from simply looking at him.

The waitress arriving with their drinks interrupted her thoughts.

"He worked hard all afternoon," she said in response to the questioning look on the woman's face.

The waitress gave her a sympathetic, comradely smile and left.

The thought that she should feel at least mildly embarrassed to have her date fall asleep crossed Emma's mind. But she didn't feel embarrassed. Instead she felt comfortable, as if sitting in this public place with Mike asleep across from her was the most natural thing in the world.

I'm simply glad I don't have to make conversation or hedge questions I don't want to answer, she told herself and ordered herself to stop staring at him and look out the window. But even though she did glance out at the night, her attention returned quickly to him.

By the time the waitress arrived with their pizza Emma was picturing herself snuggled up beside him. I need to get home and lock myself in my room before I do something really crazy, she wailed silently.

Unable to reach across the table and shake him awake without having to worry about getting into their food or spilling a drink, she slipped off her bench and onto his. "Time to wake up," she said, gently shaking his shoulder.

He moved and the muscle beneath her palm rippled. Immediately the fire his touch had ignited earlier flamed back into life. "I've heard of animal magnetism but this is a bit too much for me to accept," she muttered under her breath and quickly slipped off his bench and back onto her own as he awoke and stretched.

"Did you say something?" he asked groggily around a yawn.

"Nothing important," she replied, cautioning herself to be more careful about keeping her private thoughts private. "I suggest we just eat and go home. I have to go to work tomorrow and you look as if you could use a good night's sleep."

"This isn't how I wanted this day to end... my falling asleep on you," he said apologetically.

"Maybe it's just as well," she replied.

He frowned tiredly as if her persistent resistance was wearing him down. Maybe he'll give up, she thought. But instead of relief, this possibility caused an anxious restlessness. "I need a little time to adjust to the fact that I have found your company enjoyable," she heard herself adding.

He smiled then and her heart did another lurch. I've encouraged him, she wailed at herself. But even her self-directed anger couldn't stop the surge of pleasure that came from knowing she'd pleased him. "I just hope I don't live to rue this day," she groaned.

"Have you ever considered the possibility that some things are simply meant to be?" he asked. "Like I told you before, I've tried to respect your wishes and stay away from you. But when I realized you might marry Kenneth Drake, I felt as if a part of me would always be missing if that happened. It's as if I've never had a choice. I can't remember ever being able to ignore your presence when you were anywhere near me."

Emma stopped herself from admitting that she'd never been able to entirely ignore him, either. She'd said enough already. She needed time to think. And to do that she needed a goodly amount of distance between herself and Mike Flint. A bolted door between us wouldn't hurt, either, she added. "I'm starved," she said, abruptly changing the subject and reaching for a piece of pizza.

Impatience shadowed his features letting her know he'd hoped for a similar confession from her. Then his expression became shuttered and he, too, began to eat.

A short while later as they climbed into the cab of his truck, his continued silence began to wear on her nerves. "That pizza was terrific," she said.

"I'm glad you liked it," he replied.

Again she heard the tiredness in his voice and noticed that he had not even looked at her. Maybe, in spite of his declaration that he felt bonded to her, he'd decided she was not worth the struggle. If so, I should be relieved, she told herself. After all, without him tempting her, she could get back onto the path she'd planned for her life. But again she didn't feel relieved. Instead her nerves tensed even more.

"I really did like it," she affirmed, then mentally moaned. She was being redundant!

He looked at her then. "I'd prefer to hear you again admit that you enjoyed spending the day with me," he said gruffly.

She saw his shoulders stiffen and knew his pride was on the line. If she evaded him this time, that pride might cause him to walk away. And that is what I want, she assured herself. But when she did speak, it was her honest, disconcerted thoughts that came out. "I did . . . I do . . . I'm confused."

His expression relaxed. "I'll settle for that for now."

As he pulled out of the parking lot, again a silence fell between them but this time the tenseness was missing. That she was so acutely attuned to his moods shook Emma. But what was even more disconcerting was that several times tonight she'd had a chance to seriously discourage his interest and each time she'd encouraged him.

When they pulled up in front of her house, she grabbed the door handle. All she wanted was to escape to her room where she could be alone to think.

"I'll walk you to your door," he said, switching off the engine.

"That really isn't necessary," she assured him.

"Yes, it is."

Seeing the purposeful set to his jaw, she knew arguing would be useless. "If you insist."

"I do."

She'd climbed out of the truck by the time he came around to join her. "Will you have dinner with me tomorrow night?" he asked as they started toward the house. "I promise not to fall asleep again."

The thought that, for her, the meal would be safest if he did fall asleep played through her mind. Then she recalled how even watching him sleep had aroused fantasies that tore at the fabric of her resolve. "A part of me wants to run as far away from you as possible and never look back," she said, meeting his gaze directly.

"I can't believe you would behave so cowardly," he taunted.

She breathed a resigned sigh. "In this case, being cowardly might be the smart thing to do. You are having a very unnerving effect on me. But I'm not feeling very smart at the moment. So, yes, I'll have dinner with you."

"You've had an 'unnerving' effect on me for years." Drawing her into his arms, his mouth found hers.

Every fiber of her being seemed suddenly alive. She was vividly aware of him. Every contact held its own excitement. She'd pressed her palms against his chest, intending to keep some physical distance between them but the hard musculature had been too enticing and, instead of acting as a safeguard, her hands had moved caressingly upward to his shoulders, luxuriating in the firm feel of him.

She swayed against him and as the lengths of their bodies met, desire swept through her so intensely her knees threatened to buckle.

Panicked, she twisted free from his hold and took a step back. "We have to take this slowly," she choked out.

He frowned. "You don't have to be afraid of me. I'm not going to push you. I only want what you're freely willing to give."

"It's not you that scares me. Right at this moment, I don't trust myself." Embarrassed by this admission and still shaken by the desire he'd awakened, she started to flee toward the house.

He caught her by the arm. "I'll be by at six tomorrow evening," he said.

"Six," she repeated in confirmation, then completed her retreat into the house.

She'd meant to go straight up to her room, but instead she found herself standing at the window beside the door watching him walk back to his truck. Just the sight of him fueled the flames within. Nothing this intense can last for long, she assured herself.

Chapter Nine

Midafternoon, a little over two weeks later, Emma sat at the cash register of Balanski's Bookstore, a frown on her face. She'd been seeing Mike steadily. And she'd been wrong about the fire he'd ignited in her being so intense it would burn itself out. If anything it was even hotter.

Worse still, two nights ago, he'd had a night charter and a storm had blown through. She'd found herself pacing the living room floor just like her mother had done. Finally around one in the morning, she'd driven down to the marina. The *Reliable Lady* had been in its slip and she'd been able to get some sleep.

"You look like a woman who could use a friend to talk to," Martha's voice broke into Emma's thoughts.

"I don't know what to do about Mike Flint," Emma admitted.

Martha frowned reprimandingly. "I suppose you've discovered you were really on the rebound when you started seeing him and now you want out but you don't want to hurt him."

Emma met her employer's frown with one of her own. "No. Like I told you and everyone else, I was not on the rebound. I wasn't in love with Kenneth. I tried to convince myself that I was but the spark was missing. I'm glad he and Monica are happy."

"But you have also discovered that Mike isn't the man for you, either?" Martha prodded when Emma again fell silent.

Emma scowled. "I wish it was that simple. The problem is I don't want him to be the man for me. He's just like my father...the sea owns a large part of his heart. My instincts warned me to stay away from him... that he could be dangerous if I let him get too close. But I didn't listen. I let my barriers down. When he's around there aren't just a few sparks, there's a raging fire." She groaned. "He doesn't even have to be around. All I have to do is think about him."

Martha regarded her thoughtfully. "Did your mother ever feel shortchanged on your father's love?"

"No." Emma breathed a tired sigh. "And, the truth is, I didn't either. So he missed a few events in my life. All fathers do. Sometimes even mothers have to. And he always tried to make it up. I knew he really wanted to be there. It was the worrying I hated. The sea can be a very dangerous mistress."

"I've known a great many sailors who lived to a ripe old age. Maybe you should stop fretting and simply live your life, accepting whatever the fates have in store," Martha suggested.

Emma's jaw tensed. "I care so much it scares me."

Martha frowned impatiently and shook her head. "Some women never find that kind of passion. You should consider yourself lucky."

"It is exciting," Emma admitted, a self-conscious grin tilting one corner of her mouth.

Concern abruptly spread over Martha's face. "How does Mike feel?"

Emma could see that the proprietress was suddenly worried that Mike's feeling might not run as deeply as her own. "He's told me to let him know when I'm willing to admit that we belong together. Then we'll set the date."

Martha's expression relaxed. "And when do you think that will be? Keep in mind I'm an old woman. I can't wait forever to dance at your wedding."

Emma breathed a tired sigh. "You're right. I worry too much. Obviously my heart has a mind of its own and it's time I followed—"

The ringing of the phone interrupted.

"Balanski's Bookstore. How may I help you?" Emma said in a friendly tone as she answered.

"Emma?" a man asked over the line.

She recognized the voice. It was Paul Wooly and there was an anxiousness in his tone that caused her legs to weaken with fear. "Yes," she managed to respond.

"You need to come down to the hospital. There's been an accident. Your dad's only got a few scrapes and bruises. But Mike's hurt pretty bad."

Emma's stomach knotted so tightly she was sure she was going to be sick. "I'll be there," she said and hung up.

Martha rushed to her side and wrapped her arms around Emma's shoulders as if she was afraid the younger woman was going to fall off the stool on which she was sitting. "You look as white as a sheet."

Emma took a couple of deep breaths before she could even speak. "There's been an accident. My dad. Mike. I have to go to the hospital." Strength flowed back into her. Gently freeing herself from Martha's hold, she climbed off the stool.

Martha strode to the door and turned the Open sign to Closed. "You're in no condition to drive. I'll take you."

"Really, I'll be fine," Emma protested. "You can't close the store."

"I already have," Martha replied, turning the lock. "Now let's get going."

Realizing her hands were shaking so much she'd probably have a struggle just getting the key into the ignition, Emma swallowed a second protest and hurried to the back room to get her purse.

"They're both going to be just fine," Martha assured her as they climbed into her car.

Emma wanted to respond but she couldn't speak. It was taking all of her control not to burst into tears.

Martha glanced at her. "I'll get us there as quickly as I can."

Emma sat dumbly during the ride to the hospital. She tried not to think. When she did, she saw her father more badly injured than Paul had been willing to admit and Mike lying dying. A pain so intense she could barely breathe threatened to overwhelm her.

Martha pulled into the driveway for the Emergency entrance. "You go on in," she said. "I'll park and join you."

Emma was out of the car before Martha had finished speaking. Entering the reception area, she saw Paul.

He hurried to her. "Your dad's in here," he said, taking her by the arm and guiding her through two swinging doors and then into a room to her right. Her father was sitting on an examining table with a nurse and doctor standing beside him.

"This is his daughter," Paul said as they entered.

The young doctor turned and smiled at Emma. "Your father is going to be fine. Just a few cuts and bruises. I didn't even have to take any stitches."

Relief that Paul had been right and her father was fine swept through her. Then her gaze traveled to the second bed in the room. A bloodied sheet lay askew over it and an assortment of instruments and bandages lay scattered as if a frenzy of activity had recently occurred there. Her gaze swung back to her father and her chin trembled. "Mike?" she asked weakly.

"I'm sorry, girl." Peter eased himself off the table and put his arms around her and hugged her. "I should have listened to you."

Tears began to flow. She pushed free and looked upward. Beseeching God from the depths of her soul, she cried out with defiant anguish, "Please, he can't be dead!"

"He isn't." It was the doctor who spoke. He wrapped a comforting arm around her shoulders.

"He's in the operating room. There's a fine team of surgeons working on him."

Emma couldn't stop trembling. "How badly is he hurt?" she asked through clenched teeth as she fought to regain control.

"He has a broken arm, some injured ribs, a punctured lung. There was a bad gash in his leg. He lost a lot of blood. But he's a strong man and a fighter," he said encouragingly.

Emma turned to her father. "What happened?" she demanded.

He shook his head and tears welled up in his eyes. "It was my fault. I'm too old. I shouldn't have gone down."

"It was an accident. It would have happened no matter who had been there." Emma jerked around to see Garth Smith push back a curtain to reveal a third examining table. "I've rested long enough," the young man said, holding a hand up to the doctor to stop any protest as he joined the others. "I feel fine. Nothing happened to me."

"We found the yacht pretty close to where I said it would be," Peter spoke up, but there was no pride in his voice, merely regret. "And the water wasn't even all that deep. The storm that sunk it had carried it more toward shore than out to sea. Getting the safe seemed easy enough. Mike and Garth were going to go down and Paul and I were going to stay topside. But the excitement was too much for me. I had to see for myself. I insisted on going down with them."

"Mike didn't mind having a third hand," Garth interjected.

"But if I hadn't been there, he wouldn't have had to knock me out of the way and take the brunt of the blow himself," Peter countered, the guilt in his voice building.

"Accidents happen. That's a risk we all take," Garth insisted. He turned to Emma. "Your dad was near the bow of the boat and I was above. We were both watching for any signs of shifting or trouble. Mike went inside and found the safe. He'd attached it to the line from the boat and Paul was beginning to reel it in slowly with Mike guiding it out of the interior and into free water. It was bulky and difficult to control. Mike had gotten it clear of the cabin and gave it a tug for Paul to haul it straight up when a current caught it. The safe swung, knocking against the side railing. The hit was hard enough to cause the yacht to lurch. The boat had sunk so that it was resting in an upright position. The next thing we knew it was keeling fully over onto its side."

A look of self-disgust mingled with the guilt on Peter's face. "When I saw Mike get the safe free from the cabin, I figured the hard part was over. I got to thinking about what else we could salvage and wasn't watching what was going on."

"I figured we were home free, too," Garth said solicitously. "Truth is, I didn't even realize what was happening until I saw Mike suddenly start swimming toward your dad." His attention returned to Emma. "Mike's the only one who never assumes a job's done until it's done. He saw what was happening before either your dad or I did. Lucky for your dad, Mike was close enough to reach him and push him out from under before the boat could turn onto him. But Mike wasn't so lucky. He got clipped hard by the vessel on its way down." Garth shook his head. "It's a miracle he didn't lose his mouthpiece and suck in water. But he must have guessed he wasn't totally clear and clamped him mouth tight shut in case of an impact."

Garth paused to draw a shaky breath and fear showed on his face. Emma had the feeling he was suddenly reliving those minutes underwater. "Your dad and I got him to the surface. Lucky, too, that we weren't in such deep water we suffered any damage from not decompressing. 'Course we couldn't worry about that. Mike was bleeding pretty bad. We had to get it stopped. Even more, the blood could've brought any sharks for miles around. We had to get him into the boat."

Emma paled at the extent of the danger the men had been in.

Suddenly realizing he'd only added to her anxiousness, Garth flushed. "'Course there weren't no sharks around. And even if there had been, I had a stun stick."

Paul tossed the younger man a look that ordered him to shut up and Garth fell silent.

"I'd suggest you all go home and rest," the doctor said with command before any of the men could continue with the saga of their brush with death.

Emma faced him defiantly. "I can't leave until I know Mike's going to be all right."

"I'm not leaving, either," Peter insisted.

"None of us is leaving." Paul and Garth spoke up in unison.

A plea entered Emma's voice. "We're the closest to family he has here in Clover or anywhere for several thousand miles."

The doctor's gaze traveled over the anxious, determined faces staring at him and he nodded. "All right. I'll take you to the waiting room and tell the surgeon to let you know as soon as they know anything."

"What's going on?" Martha asked, joining the quartet as they followed the doctor out of the emergency area.

"They're operating on Mike," Emma informed her, the words barely getting out around the lump in her throat.

Martha fell silently into step with the others as they continued to the waiting area.

When the doctor left them to begin their vigil, Peter placed an arm around Emma's shoulders. "I'm sorry, girl," he said again. "Mike almost got killed and we didn't even get the damn safe. There wasn't time to bring it aboard. We had to cut it loose and get Mike to shore as quickly as possible. Looks like he risked his life for nothing."

"Mike Flint is made out of the same cloth you are," she replied. "What happened was not your fault. It wasn't anyone's fault. It's the way you choose to live your lives." She turned and gave him a hug. "I'm glad you're all right. And Mike will be, too." Her jaw firmed with determination. "He has to be. We have some unfinished business. Now you sit down and rest or I'll ask Martha to take you home. And you know how insistent she can be."

Peter gave her another hug, then seated himself.

Wishing she was as positive of Mike's recovery as she'd sounded when she'd spoken to her father, Emma told herself to sit down as well, but she was too tense. Instead she wandered to the window and stood staring out with unseeing eyes.

"Are you all right?"

Emma glanced to her side to see that Martha had joined her. "This was exactly why I didn't want to fall in love with Mike Flint," she said tiredly. Her gaze again shifted to the view beyond the window. "You would think this would convince me that I was right and should walk away from him." Tears welled in her eyes and she turned back to Martha. "Instead I find myself furious that I didn't marry him sooner... that I don't have more memories to carry with me if he should die."

Martha took Emma's hand in hers. "He'll be fine. We have to believe that."

Emma merely nodded as her chin trembled and one of the tears she'd been fighting to hold back escaped and trickled down her cheek.

An hour later Emma felt as if she could literally climb the walls. Never had time passed so slowly. The three men in the room with her looked exhausted. Martha had gone and gotten coffee and sandwiches but no one had taken more than a bite or two.

The sound of the door opening brought Emma around with a jerk. Her breath locked in her lungs when she saw the grim expression on the surgeon's face. Don't panic, she ordered herself. "Can we see Mike?" The words came out more as a demand than a request.

"Are any of you immediate family?" the doctor asked.

Emma felt the bile rise in her throat.

"We're as close to family as he has here in Clover," Peter replied, parroting Emma's earlier words. "Anyone else is better than a couple of thousand miles away."

The doctor's expression became masked. "I'm not certain when he'll be able to have visitors."

Emma saw the shadow of uneasiness in his eyes and her stomach knotted until she thought she might double over in pain.

"Mr. Flint has survived the operation," the surgeon continued. "He had a broken arm and a couple of fractured ribs. One of the ribs punctured a lung but we've repaired the damage and set the bones. The gash in his leg was deep but that's been closed as well."

"And he's going to be just fine," Paul added encouragingly, clearly hoping the doctor would say these words.

The grimness on the medical man's face deepened. "He lost a lot of blood. He fought hard to stay with us but he's slipped into a coma."

Afraid that if she did open her mouth a wail of agony would issue, Emma stood mutely.

"He'll come out of it," Paul declared.

"Of course he will," Martha concurred.

Garth nodded. "I've never known Mike Flint to just lie around wasting his time."

"He's never been one to let moss grow under his feet," Peter added.

The doctor smiled encouragingly. "We're doing everything we can. But it could be days before we know anything. Looks to me like the rest of you could use some rest. Why don't you go on home. You can leave your phone numbers with the nurse at the desk and we'll let you know if there's any change in his condition."

"I don't feel right about leaving," Paul said, looking like a man caught between a rock and a hard place. "But we do have a charter tomorrow and I should get the boat swabbed. He'd expect me to keep the business going."

"Yes, he would. He won't appreciate waking up to bankruptcy," Emma said, breaking her silence, and marveled that she could sound so calm. Her gaze shifted to Garth. "You need to go home and get some rest as well." This came out more as an order than a suggestion. Then her attention turned to her father and Martha. "Someone should stay. I'll be that someone. Martha would you take my father home?"

"We'll stay with you," Peter spoke up quickly.

Emma's jaw firmed with resolve. "If you don't get some rest, you're going to get sick. Besides, I need some time alone."

Martha nodded knowingly. "Come along," she said, ushering the others out ahead of her. As they started down the hall, she glanced back at Emma. "Call me if you need a friend to sit with you," she said.

Emma forced a smile. "Thanks. Just get my dad home. I'll be fine."

Martha unexpectedly turned back and gave her a hug. "Both you and Mike will be fine," she said with certainty, then quickly led the men out.

"I wish I could be that certain," Emma muttered under her breath.

She waited until the others had left the floor, then knew she could wait no longer. She had to see Mike even if it meant fighting her way through a throng of nurses and doctors. Approaching the nurse on duty, she said, "I need to see Mike Flint."

The nurse looked up, sympathy on her face. "He's in intensive care. Only family is allowed in there."

"I'm as close to family as he has here," Emma insisted. A thought occurred to her. "I'm his fiancée."

The nurse looked uncertain.

"I've heard that talking to someone in a coma can help them come out of it," Emma persisted. "Please, you have to let me see him."

"I can't make that decision," the nurse replied. For a moment she hesitated, then reached for her phone. "I'll call the doctor."

Emma stood impatiently waiting while the nurse made the call and the sound of the doctor being paged issued from the hospital intercom system. When Emma saw him coming down the hall, she met him halfway. "I have to see Mike," she said, determination in her voice. "I'm his fiancée. I've seen shows on television where people continually talk to patients in comas and their talking brings the person back. You have to let me try to get through to him."

He frowned as if he was going to reject her plea. Then his expression softened. "It can't hurt to let you try," he conceded. His voice took on a fatherly tone. "Come with me."

Emma followed him into a room filled with various pieces of equipment. One wall was plate glass and looked onto a nurses' station that housed a battery of monitoring screens. Inside the room Mike was lying in a bed hooked up to the partner devices that would trigger a reaction on the nurses' screens should his condition change. To Emma's relief there were no other patients in the room at the moment.

"If you need any assistance, push this button," the doctor instructed, showing her a red button on the wall.

"Thank you," she muttered, barely hearing his words. Her attention was on Mike. He looked so lifeless she again had to fight down the urge to panic. The heart monitor showed a slow but steady rhythm. Still, she watched his chest to make certain he was really breathing. The rise and fall was minimal but it was there.

Wanting privacy before she spoke, she glanced up to make certain the doctor had left and they were alone. Then her full attention returned to Mike. Standing beside his bed, her gaze bore into him. "Don't you dare die on me, Mike Flint," she said curtly. "You made me realize I love you. It isn't fair for you to leave me now."

As if she could will her own strength into him, she closed both her hands around his hand and held on tight. "You asked me to marry you and I intend to see that you live to fulfill that commitment."

His hand encased in hers continued to feel limp. She searched his face and saw no sign that he'd heard her. Her legs felt shaky. Not willing to release his hand, she continued to hold tight to him as she sank into the chair beside the bed. Studying his gaunt features, her jaw firmed. "I am not going to let you slip away from me," she said tersely. She drew a steadying breath, then continued in gentler tones. "I've been thinking about the house you want to build outside of town. It should be large enough for a family. I think you're right, two children would be nice."

As Emma continued describing the rooms she wanted in the house, she pictured herself there with Mike and their children. The image felt right as if this was what was meant to be.

For a long time she talked, all the while searching his face for any sign he heard her. But again there was none. Exhaustion caused by her worry made her groggy. She laid her head on her hands, which still held his.

"Miss?"

Emma jerked awake. She'd only meant to rest a moment. A glance at her watch told her she'd been asleep an hour.

"Maybe you should go home and get some rest," the nurse who had woken her suggested. "I'll call you if there's any change."

Releasing her hold on Mike, Emma stretched her back and rubbed at the stiffness in her neck. "I can't leave," she said.

"You're not going to do him any good if you get yourself sick from worry," the nurse coaxed.

"I can't leave," Emma repeated. When she had finally admitted that she loved Mike, she hadn't realized how strong a bond that emotion was within her. Now she felt as if a part of her was lying in that bed.

"Would you like something to eat or drink?" the nurse offered, giving up her attempt to convince Emma to go.

"Some water," Emma requested, the thought of anything else causing her stomach to churn.

The nurse brought her a pitcher and a glass, then finished checking the machine attachments to Mike and noting his vital signs on the chart at the end of the bed. "Ring if you need me," she said as she headed for the door.

"Thanks," Emma replied to her departing back.

Rising and standing beside the bed, she again studied the lines of his face. They seemed more gaunt than before. The tears she'd been holding back flooded her eyes and began to spill out down her cheeks. "Damn you, Mike Flint! Don't do this to me. Open your eyes! Come back to me!"

Her shoulders shook as she fought to cry quietly, holding in the sobs that wanted to burst from her. "I didn't want you in my life but you insisted. Now I can't imagine life without you."

"Emma," a groggy male voice murmured.

A gasp of surprise escaped and she frantically attempted to blink the tears from her eyes. Her vision still blurred, she looked hard at his face. His eyes were still closed and for a moment she was afraid that she'd wanted him to wake so badly she was imagining things. She rubbed her eyes, attempting to clear her vision more, then peered hard at him. "Mike?" she said his name shakily.

"Emma," he repeated and this time his eyes opened slowly to half slits.

"You're going to be all right," she stated firmly. Fresh tears rolled down her cheeks only this time they were tears of relief. She pressed the button for the nurse, then gently caressed his jaw.

"I guess this is one of those times you'd hoped to avoid by staying away from me," he murmured, the words coming out slurred.

"It has been a bit trying but I lived through it," she replied.

The hurried opening of the door caught her attention. "He's awake," she announced as the nurse entered.

The woman in white smiled. "I'll call the doctor," she said, picking up the phone on the wall.

"I feel tired," Mike muttered and closed his eyes.

"Don't you drift away from me again," Emma ordered.

"I'm just going to sleep a little," he replied.

The nurse had approached the bed. "His pulse is stronger and his breathing is deeper," she announced happily. "He is just sleeping now."

Several hours later, Emma eased herself into the recliner in Mike's hospital room. The doctor had kept him in intensive care for a while longer to make certain he was not going to lapse back into a coma. The staff had tried to convince Emma to go home and get some rest, but she'd insisted on staying and they'd allowed her to.

While Mike was being disconnected from the machines and taken to his room, she'd called her father. The nurse, she knew, had called earlier but she wanted to reassure him and make certain the others had been called and told that Mike had awakened. Then she'd hurried up to Mike's room, driven by the fear that if she wasn't standing guard over him, he might slip away from her again.

Now as she sat watching him sleep, she remembered something her mother had once said that she'd never quite understood. It was late one night. Her father had been out on a charter and an unexpected storm had blown up the coast. Her mother had been sitting in a chair in the living room, almost, it seemed, in a trance.

"Are you all right?" Emma had asked, the vacant look on her mother's face frightening her.

Nancy Wynn had blinked as if startled to discover another presence in the room, then smiled reassuringly at her daughter. "I was just willing your father back to me," she said. "I've always had the feeling that if both our wills are set on the same purpose, together we can pull each other through the worst of storms."

And that was how she felt at that moment, Emma realized. With her will locked to Mike's, he could not be taken from her.

For a long time, she sat simply watching him, glad he was resting but eager to speak to him again when he woke. Finally, exhaustion again overwhelmed her and she slept.

She awoke to the sound of voices. It was the nurse and Mike.

"It's nice to see you back in the world of the living, Mr. Flint," the woman in white said as she removed a thermometer from his mouth and then noted the results on his chart.

Emma rose and moved to the bed. "It certainly is," she confirmed, gently touching his cheek.

Mike's gaze narrowed on her. "You've been here all night?"

Realizing she must look a mess, Emma raked a hand self-consciously through her hair. "I needed to be certain you didn't fade out on me again."

The nurse smiled. "He looks like a man on his way to a speedy recovery," she asserted as she finished making notations on his chart. Then hanging it on the foot of the bed, she left.

"I'm sorry to have put you through this," he apologized as soon as they were alone.

"You can't have highs without experiencing a few lows," Emma returned philosophically.

"Thanks for being here," he said drowsily.

Emma saw his eyelids slowly lowering and knew he was fighting to remain awake. Catching a glimpse of herself in the mirror, she grimaced. She looked worse than he did. The crying had left circles under her eyes and her features looking drawn. Her clothes were a bundle of wrinkles and her hair looked like a fright wig. Maybe I had better go home and clean up before he begins to wonder if I always look this bad in the morning, she joked silently to herself. Aloud, she said softly, "You rest. I'll be back later."

His eyes opened once again. "I'm sorry, Emma," he said. "I never realized what a strain worrying about someone else could be." Then he closed his eyes and slept.

Chapter Ten

Emma sat at the kitchen table frowning into her coffee. It was Monday... the fifth day since Mike's accident. The first couple of days he'd been heavily drugged with painkillers. On Saturday, he'd been more clearheaded and awake.

But this had been her Saturday to work and none of Martha's usual part-time help could come in. Emma hadn't wanted Martha trying to handle the store alone, so she hadn't been able to get to the hospital until the evening visiting hours. By the time she arrived, Garth and her father were already there. She'd been tempted to ask them to leave so she could have some time alone with Mike, but this was the first time they'd been allowed in to see him and she knew they needed to reassure themselves that he was going to be fine.

Just when she was sure they were leaving and she was going to have some private time with Mike, Paul arrived. In the end, she'd had to beg an extra minute from the floor nurse to have a moment alone with him.

She'd considered waiting until he was out of the hospital to tell him of her decision, then decided that she didn't want to wait. Now that she'd faced the depth of her feelings for him, she wanted to be his wife as soon as possible. Standing beside his bed, she'd grinned self-consciously. "If seeing me when you first woke from your comma didn't scare you too badly, we can start making plans for our wedding as soon as you're out of here," she'd said.

"Seeing you is always a pleasure," he'd replied with an answering smile.

She'd flushed with joy.

The floor nurse had stuck her head in the door at that moment. "You really have to leave now," she insisted with apology.

"I'll be back tomorrow," Emma had promised as she placed a light kiss on his lips, then she'd left.

But yesterday when she and Peter had gone to visit, Mike's reception hadn't been what she'd expected. He'd seemed distracted.

She'd waited to tell her father that she'd finally accepted Mike's proposal. She thought she and Mike would tell him together. But Mike never brought up the subject.

At first she'd been puzzled, then the reason for his behavior had dawned on her. He was planning to go back after the safe and he was worried about her reaction. I suppose he thinks I'll call off the wedding, she'd thought. And, she had to admit, the prospect of him going back for the safe had sent a chill of dread through her.

When visiting hours ended, he'd confirmed this suspicion. Her father and the others had left and she'd lagged behind to give him a kiss in private. His lips had felt almost wooden and he'd caught her by the hand before she could move away from the bed.

"We have to talk," he'd said grimly.

"We will," she'd replied, already knowing that she would bite back any protest she considered making when he told her he was returning for the safe. They could never be happy unless she accepted him as he was and did not try to change him or harness him.

However, as she stared into her coffee this Monday morning, the image of him lying in the hospital bed taunted her and a plan that had begun fermenting in her mind the evening before grew in strength. Since she'd worked on Saturday, today was her day off. And her father had no charter scheduled.

"You look like someone with something important on your mind," Peter said, breaking the silence that had been hanging over the kitchen for the past several minutes.

"I do," she replied. "When Mike mends, I know he'll want to go back for that safe."

"Most likely," he confirmed.

"I think we should go get it now. Paul said yesterday that he didn't have a charter lined up for today and I'm a good diver. We just need to convince Garth's dad that he should let his son off for the day."

"I don't think Mike would approve," Peter cautioned.

Emma smiled mischievously. "Then we won't tell him. We'll say that you and Paul got charters after all and I went along to crew for you because you couldn't find anyone else. That'll explain why we're going to miss the afternoon visiting hours." Before her father could protest, she was on her way to the phone.

Paul was equally sure Mike wouldn't approve of Emma leading a team down to get the safe. But when she said she was going to go with or without him, he agreed to go.

Garth was easy to convince. He'd already begun to worry about the safe shifting position or being covered by the silt from the bottom, making it difficult to find. He promised to meet her at the marina within the hour.

Later, as they left the marina behind and headed out to sea, she saw the relief and excitement in her father's and Paul's eyes and knew that they'd been anxious to recover the safe as well. The split of the profits, she'd insisted, would remain the same as it had been originally set up. Each of the men and Mike would receive a fourth. She was simply along for the ride.

Standing by the rail, she breathed in deeply of the sea air. The same excitement she'd seen in the men's eyes welled up in her. Even the element of danger didn't seem to be dampening her spirits. It seemed, in fact, to add a certain zest. Seating herself on one of the benches along the rail, she leaned back and let the sun warm her. This was fun, she admitted. The thought that once she and Mike were married, she might quit her job at the bookstore and help him run his business played through her mind. Perhaps she had a little more seawater in her blood than she'd been willing to admit, she mused silently.

As they neared the spot where they'd found the wreck before, they scanned the horizon for any other ships. To their relief, they would have no competition.

Climbing into her diving gear, Emma grinned with anticipation. But as she, her father and Garth prepared to enter the water, the image of Mike lying in a hospital bed filled her mind. "Be careful," she ordered her two companions.

Both nodded solemnly, then one at a time they fell back into the cool depths.

It took them nearly an hour to find the safe. But the rest of the recovery went smoothly. When the safe was finally hoisted on board and secured, all four let out a cheer of accomplishment.

"I think Emma should have the pleasure of telling Mike," Paul suggested. And the others concurred.

That night Emma took pains to look her most feminine. She chose a low-cut cotton dress and white sandals. Fairly glowing with excitement, she entered Mike's room.

His smile of greeting looked forced and the tired lines under his eyes seemed deeper as if he hadn't been sleeping well. Concern that he was not healing as quickly as the doctor had predicted swept through her. "How are you feeling?" she asked, approaching the bed and studying his face searchingly.

"I'm feeling a hundred percent better. The doctor says I should be able to leave tomorrow. I'll have to take it easy for a while until my bones mend. But that'll give me time to catch up on my paperwork.''

"And plan a wedding," she added, promising herself that she would make certain he followed the doctor's orders.

His expression grew grim. "About that wedding..."

He hesitated and Emma felt her stomach knotting. Instinctively she knew she wasn't going to like what he was about to say.

"This experience has caused me to do some thinking about my life. I'm not ready to settle down just yet," he said stiffly.

Emma felt as if she'd received a physical blow. Unconsciously she took a step back. Her hands balled into fists as she fought to hold back the hot tears burning at the back of her eyes. Then the truth dawned on her and humiliation swept through her. "I was a challenge. That was all I was to you."

He watched her, his expression shuttered. "You never wanted to marry a seafaring man. You should think of this as a welcome escape."

What a fool she'd been! "I will," she snarled, and turned and strode from the room.

"It wasn't the treasure that had him acting so preoccupied, it was getting rid of me," she muttered as she drove home.

Tears began to trickle down her cheeks. Angrily she brushed them away. "I will not cry over a cad!" she seethed.

Her father was in the kitchen when she arrived. "You're home early," he greeted her with surprise. "I know how lousy hospital food is. I was just packing a picnic dinner with my famous ham and swiss on pumpernickel sandwiches. I even went by Peg's and picked up one of her chocolate pies. Thought I'd give you a while alone with Mike and then I'd bring this food over and we'd celebrate.''

"You can go celebrate with Mr. Flint. If I never see him again, I'll die a happy woman," she tossed over her shoulder, continuing through the kitchen and into the hall.

Peter caught up with her at the foot of the stairs. Laying a hand on her arm, he brought her to a halt. "Girl, what's wrong?" For the first time he got a look at her face. "You're as pale as a ghost." He studied her worriedly. "Don't tell me you and Mike had a fight about us going after the safe. I was sure once he found out we'd gotten it, he'd be pleased.''

"I never got a chance to tell him about the safe," she replied through clenched teeth, her anger building to a fury.

"Then what happened?" he demanded.

"I told him a couple of days ago, I'd decided to accept his offer of marriage." Making this admission aloud was humiliating but she forced herself to go on. "He seemed preoccupied but I was sure it was the safe that was on his mind." Against her will, tears again welled in her eyes. "I was wrong. It seems his near-death experience had caused him to reexamine his goals in life and he'd decided that being married to me was no longer one of them.''

"That bastard," Peter growled. "The man should be blessing his angels to have you as a wife.''

"He can do whatever he wants. I don't give a hoot. Just don't ever mention his name in front of me again." Feeling the tears threatening to escape and not wanting anyone to see her cry even angry tears over a scoundrel like Mike Flint, she held her head with dignity and continued up the stairs.

As she reached the upper floor, she heard the front door slam. The realization that her father was probably on his way to the hospital to give Mike a piece of his mind, caused her to whirl around and race back downstairs and outside. She was too late. His car was halfway down the road by the time she reached the porch.

"That's all I need . . . a shouting match between my father and Mike Flint in the hospital so that all the world will know I've been jilted." Tears of anger poured down her cheeks. "I was such a fool! This is one lesson I won't forget!"

Storming back inside, she went upstairs. In spite of her anger there was still a deep hurt. Furious with herself for having cared for a man who had turned out to be so shallow, she brushed annoyedly at her tears. "I will not cry another drop over this," she growled and blinked the remainder of the wetness from her eyes.

Reaching up to massage the taut muscles of her neck, she thought of a bubble bath. "Just what I need to relax me and wash that man out of my mind," she announced aloud and headed for the bathroom.

"Everyone gets made a fool of at least once in their life," she philosophized a little later as she lay in the hot water. "And if I'd stuck to my original course, this never would have happened." Resolve etched itself into her features. "From now on, logic will be my guide."

A knock sounded on the bathroom door. "Are you all right, girl?" Her father's voice sounded through the barrier.

"I'm fine," she called back.

"Taking a bubble bath?" he asked, adding in gentle tones, "Your mom used to do that whenever she was upset."

Refusing to admit she was still allowing Mike Flint to affect her, she forced a tone of nonchalance into her voice. "I'm not upset any longer. That dive today left me a little sore."

"That's my girl," he said approvingly. His voice took on a harsh edge. "I had a talk with Mike."

Emma groaned and sank lower in the water. "I hope it wasn't a shouting match for all the hospital to hear."

"We kept it private," he assured her.

"At least I can be grateful for that," she murmured, continuing to remain low in the water and wishing she'd never allowed Mike Flint into her life.

"You're better off without him," her father continued. "You'll find yourself some nice landlubber and raise a passel of kids."

"Absolutely," she called back. As she heard him walking away, to herself she added, "There might not be any rockets with red glares but there won't be any crash landings, either."

Chapter Eleven

"So it's over between Mike and me. I was simply a challenge he couldn't resist. Once he'd won, he was no longer interested," Emma concluded. Knowing that she was going to have to tell Martha sooner or later what had happened, Emma had gone in early to work the following morning so she could relate her news in private.

Martha shook her head in disbelief. "I just can't believe he acted like such a…" She paused for lack of the proper word.

"Heel. Cad. Scoundrel. Lout. Reprobate. Jerk. Rat." Emma offered a few of the descriptions she'd come up with while she'd dressed that morning.

"All of the above," Martha replied.

"What I can't believe is I was such a dupe. I trusted him. I thought he was being honest with me." Emma's anger at herself rekindled.

"He had me fooled as well," Martha soothed. "He has everyone in town fooled. Why if you ask anyone who thinks they know him well, they'll tell you he's the most honest, straightforward man they know."

"He is one terrific actor," Emma conceded. "But at least he's now out of my life for good. Which was what I wanted in the first place."

"Men." Martha shook her head as if speaking of an entity that was totally incomprehensible. Suddenly her eyes brightened. "However, it's always been my theory that if you fall off a horse, the only cure is to climb right back on. The new history teacher at the high school was in again yesterday. And he's still unattached."

"And I think I'll stay unattached for a while," Emma said firmly, letting her employer know she wasn't interested in any matchmaking Martha might be considering.

"I suppose a short cooling-off period wouldn't hurt," Martha conceded, then went to unlock the door and open the store for business.

Two days later Emma returned home from work, sank onto the couch, kicked off her shoes and put her feet up on the coffee table. Wiggling her toes to ease the soreness of having been on her feet for nearly eight hours, she frowned musingly.

The news of her breakup with Mike had spread. The irony was that everyone thought she was the one who had jilted him. She recalled her encounter with Mayabelle Appleton today at the store.

Emma had seen Mayabelle coming in her direction with a purposeful expression on her face and tried to escape to the back room. But Mayabelle had been surprisingly fast for a woman her age and had literally cornered Emma. "I can understand how you feel, dear," she'd said, blocking Emma's retreat by standing in the center of a dead-end aisle so that Emma could not get around her. "That Mike Flint nearly got himself killed on this latest escapade and you know he's going to turn around and do something equally dangerous in the near future. You're much wiser to go looking for a more stable sort of man."

"I intend to," Emma had assured her and Mayabelle had nodded with approval and strode away with a smile on her face.

Leaning back on the couch, Emma combed her hair back with her fingers. She was fairly certain that Mike was the one who had made everyone believe she was the one who'd broken off their relationship. "I suppose I should be grateful to him for leaving me some pride," she mumbled. Again self-directed anger filled her. He'd fooled her completely and she would not feel grateful to him for anything! "He's just playing the injured party so people won't see him for the cad he is," she seethed.

The sound of her father's car pulling into the driveway caught her attention and she wondered if Roland Meldon had actually showed up today to claim his safe. She heard her father whistling and guessed he had.

Peter entered the living room waving a check. "It was just like the man said," he told her. "He opened the safe right in front of us. He didn't pay no heed to most of the papers but just pulled out a packet of photographs and a couple of leather-bound volumes and checked to make certain there had been no damage.''

Peter grinned. ''He actually clutched one of the books to his chest. 'These are the records of my travels and thoughts for the past two years,' he says as if he was holding gold in his hands. 'I've recorded my life since the age of ten. Even after I'm dead, a part of me will remain through my thoughts and words.''' Peter shook his head. ''Never seen a man so excited about assuring his immortality by way of a bunch of books that will probably bore the readers to death.''

''They could be interesting...gossip about friends, thoughts on current issues in the news,'' Emma suggested.

Peter shook his head. ''He let me look at one. One whole page was devoted to how he chose the clothes he was going to wear that morning, the weather and what he ate for breakfast.''

Emma made a face at the thought of the man's ego. Then in all fairness, she said, ''They will probably be of great use to archaeologists and historians in the future.''

''So long as those archaeologists and historians don't try to say we all lived like that.'' Peter grimaced. ''The man ate pureed prunes topped with whipped cream.''

Emma laughed lightly at the face her father made.

''It's good to see you smiling again, girl,'' he said. Then reaching into his pocket, he pulled out a second check. ''Mike insisted on signing his portion over to you.''

Emma stiffened and her smile vanished. ''He did what?''

Peter extended the check toward her. "He wanted you to have it. Mr. Meldon insisted on paying all the medical bills from the accident over and above the reward, so Mike said he figured he came out even."

Emma glared at the check. "I don't want it. It belongs to Mike Flint and I don't want anything that has to do with him."

Her father nodded. "I told him that's what you'd say but he was real insistent. He said you were part of the group who actually retrieved the safe so you should have the reward."

"Well, you can just take it right back to him." Emma pushed herself hard against the back of the couch to put more distance between herself and the unwanted piece of paper as her father extended the check even closer to her.

For a moment Peter Wynn seemed indecisive, then he straightened to his full height and looked down at her. "He's got his mind set on this. If you want the check returned, you're going to have to take it to him yourself."

Emma stared at her father in shock. "You actually want me to speak to that heel personally?"

"I know what he did seemed cruel," he said. "But I honestly believe he does have your best interests at heart."

Emma couldn't believe her ears. She glared at her father, but behind the anger her hurt showed. "He made a fool out of me and you're siding with him?"

Peter Wynn laid the check on the coffee table and approached his daughter. "I have always and will always be on *your* side," he assured her. He kissed her lightly on the forehead. "I'll broil us some fish for dinner."

As he left, Emma sat staring at the check. "Mr. Mike Flint is obviously trying to buy off a guilty conscience," she mused with disgust. But the fact that he had a guilty conscience didn't make him less a heel.

Well, maybe a little less, her fair side admitted. And there was the possibility he had actually thought he was in love with her up to the moment she accepted his proposal. After all, she had known him all her life and she'd never known him to be a man who played games with other people's emotions.

"I just wish he'd stayed away from mine," she growled. Her gaze narrowed on the check. That he thought she could be bought enraged her.

Rising from the couch, she grabbed up the check and headed to the kitchen. "I'm going to return this money to Mike Flint and this time I plan to make it absolutely clear that I don't want him even casting his shadow in my direction."

Peter Wynn grinned with approval. "It won't hurt him to learn you're a lot tougher than you look."

Emma nodded and continued out the back door.

The front door of Mike's house was open, allowing the fresh breeze in through the screen door. Emma pressed the bell and heard it ring.

"Come in." Mike's voice sounded from the interior.

She hadn't wanted to even enter his house. But maybe going inside would be better, she reasoned, catching a glimpse of movement across the street and realizing Mayabelle Appleton had stepped out onto her porch.

Opening the screen door, Emma entered the front hall.

"I'm in the living room." Mike called out.

The memory of the last evening they'd spent here flooded into her mind. He'd cooked dinner and she'd kidded him about his surprisingly adept domestic side.

"I'd like the chance to prove to you I can be adept at other things as well," he'd said with a playful leer as he'd drawn her into his arms, then kissed her with a passion that had set her body on fire.

Furious with herself for even allowing this memory to emerge, she shoved it back to the dark recesses of her mind. Just get this over with and get out of here, she ordered herself.

Entering the living room, she saw him seated in one of the large, comfortable upholstered chairs near the fireplace.

Surprise showed on his face. "I would have come to the door but my leg's been bothering me," he apologized, clumsily rising to his feet.

"No need to get up on my account," she said. In spite of the renewed anger his presence evoked, she experienced a rush of concern for him. His movement had brought pain lines to his face. Even without them, he looked pale and gaunt.

His expression became shuttered. "I needed to stretch a little anyway," he replied, remaining standing.

"I just came by to return this." She pulled the check out of her pocket and laid it on the coffee table.

He scowled at the piece of paper, then turned his gaze on her. "You deserve it. You were one of the four who actually recovered the safe," he insisted.

She glared at him. "My goodwill cannot be bought, Mr. Flint! You played me for a fool. I don't want you ever crossing my path again and that includes anything that has to do with you including your portion of the reward." Having said her piece, she turned to leave.

"Just for the record, I didn't play you for a fool," he growled at her departing back. "I did care for you. I still care about you. I want you to have a good life."

Emma swung around, disbelief etched into her features. "I suppose you're going to tell me next that during your 'near death' experience you saw God and he told you you had a mission on this earth and that mission didn't include marrying me," she returned sarcastically.

For a long moment he regarded her in a terse silence as if holding a mental debate with himself. Then he said gruffly, "What I saw was the tears, the exhaustion and the anxiety on your face when I first opened my eyes. I couldn't get that image out of my mind. For the first time, I realized the pain you'd been trying to avoid by avoiding me all these years. I did what I thought was best for you."

Emma stood mutely staring at him. Remarks her father had made suddenly made sense. "So for my own good you chose to jilt me."

His frown deepened. "I considered going into another line of work but, as you've so often pointed out, the sea is in my blood. I'd be miserable pursuing some other occupation."

Emma was stunned. He'd actually contemplated giving up the sea for her! "I can't imagine you as a landlubber," she said.

He nodded. "I came to the conclusion that marrying you would be selfish of me."

Anger at him again flared. "And so you decided this all on your own as if I was too immature to have any say in my own future."

"I knew the kind of life I could offer you was not what you honestly wanted."

"A woman can change her mind."

Hope flashed in his eyes. "Emma?" he spoke her name questioningly as if afraid he hadn't heard her right.

"The life I'd pictured for myself seems bland and boring now," she admitted.

He took a step toward her, then stopped and studied her narrowly. "Are you sure?"

"I've never been so sure of what I want." A sheepishness came over her features. "The truth is I understand now how you feel about the sea. I've discovered I've got a little more seawater in my veins than I realized."

He grinned with relief. "In that case, Emma Wynn, will you marry me?"

The urge to rush into his arms was strong, but she held herself back. "Before I answer, I want your word you won't make any more decisions for me without consulting me first," she bargained.

"Never again," he promised, his smile warming until she could feel the heat like a physical touch.

"Then my answer is yes," she said moving to him.

Wrapping his uninjured arm around her, he crushed her to him. "I've been so lonely without you. When I slept, I dreamt of you and I'd wake up feeling like a part of me was missing."

Emma looked up into his haggard features. "I'd suggest we sit down before you fall down," she said, kissing him lightly on the lips as she spoke.

He nodded in agreement and, releasing her from his embrace, took her by the hand and led her to the couch. "I've been having a recurring image of you, me and two children," he said as they sat down and he again drew her close.

"And a big two-story house with a balcony off the master bedroom?" she asked.

He nodded, then added, "On my property by the river."

Emma grinned with pleasure. So her voice had reached him even when he'd seemed more dead than alive. She snuggled more closely against him. "I know that house well and I'm sure we'll be very happy there."

"I'm sure we will, too," he replied with a kiss that promised a lifetime of love.

"I know that glow," Katie said as Emma mounted the porch steps of The Clover Street Boarding House.

Emma flushed with happiness.

"Yes, it's definitely love," Katie teased, setting aside the oilcan she'd been using to lubricate the hinge on the screen door.

"Mike and I have set the date," Emma confirmed her friend's evaluation. "Martha's going to be my maid of honor. I'd like for you to be one of my bridesmaids."

"Always a bridesmaid," Katie mused playfully.

Behind her friend's banter, Emma was sure she saw a flash of pain.

Then the momentary darkness was gone. Grinning brightly, Katie gave Emma a hug. "I wouldn't miss your wedding for the world. I'd love to stand with you."

"Someday your Mr. Right will come along," Emma assured her as she returned the hug.

A distant look came into Katie's eyes. "Maybe." Then the shadow vanished and her smile returned. "However, until then, come inside. I'll brew us a pot of coffee and you can tell me all about your wedding plans."

Hoping her friend would someday find the same happiness she'd found, Emma accompanied Katie inside.

*   *   *   *   *

Don't miss the next book
in Silhouette's exciting
ALWAYS A BRIDESMAID series.

Here's a sneak preview of

THE BACHELOR PARTY

by Paula Detmer Riggs

available in August from
Silhouette Intimate Moments.

Chapter One

For the moment they were safe.

Sophie Reynolds sank down on the bed and cradled her daughter, Jessamine, close to her breast. Exhausted and scared, she waited for the sound of retreating footsteps to fade before allowing herself to relax.

The Clover Street Boarding House wasn't plush, but the room she'd just rented was large, airy and very clean with plenty of room for the crib she would need to buy. Best of all, the first week's rent hadn't completely depleted her meager funds.

Before she'd left Portland, she'd spent endless hours reinventing the bare bones past of a woman named Sophie Reynolds. And then, one by one, she had added enough details to make the past believable. It wasn't all pretense. She was a widow, and she was twenty-eight. But she wasn't from Billings, Montana, and she hadn't spent the last year keeping house for an elderly rancher in a neighboring town.

"We're safe now, Jess," she whispered, watching the baby's face closely for a sign she was coming to know her mother's voice. "No one will find us here, I promise. And if anyone gets suspicious, we'll just move on."

Jessie's tiny fingers opened and closed against her hand, and her brown eyes looked up at her with perfect trust. Sophie's chest swelled with love.

Nothing was more important than Jessie. Not the words uttered by some coldhearted judge in Portland courtrooms, not the determination of dispassionate officers of the law sworn to enforce those words.

Without Jessie, she had no life, no reason to open her eyes every morning, no hope. No matter what hardships she had to face, or what lies she had to tell, she would never let anyone take her child from her again.

Three months later...

It was six-twenty on a raw Monday morning in early December when Sophie felt the air change and knew that Sheriff Fort Maguire had just walked into Peg's Diner.

She'd been working at Peg's for nearly three months now, and just about every morning at twenty past six he walked through the front door, looking grumpy and intensely male in his crisp khaki uniform, his stride more swagger than hurry, and a small gold badge glittering on the left side of his wide chest, just above his heart.

To her dismay Sophie was finding it difficult to dislike the man, even though he was a living, breathing, intensely masculine symbol of all that she feared. Something about the way he kept part of himself distant from others, even when he joined in the morning banter, had touched her deeply—like the lone wolf who patrolled the perimeter of the camp on the darkest, coldest nights so that those he guarded stayed warm and safe.

No matter how drawn to him she might find herself, however, she needed to remember that he was an officer of the law, and therefore, a man to be avoided at all costs.

Grabbing a quick breath, Sophie reached for the coffeepot and turned to greet him as he sat himself at the counter. "Coffee, Sheriff?"

"Yes, ma'am," he said as she poured him a cup, admiring both her face and figure. "Looks like you've done this kind of work before."

"A few times."

"Close by, or up north?"

"In Montana," Sophie replied. "I'm from Billings."

Ford figured most folks wouldn't have noticed the split second hesitation before she'd answered. He'd noticed because it was his job to notice. He didn't figure it mattered much why she had trouble with the question. Still, it didn't hurt to file that fact away.

"Findin' Peg pretty demanding, are you?" he asked.

"A little, but I like to know exactly what my employer expects." Her smile was restrained, her answer cautious. He understood caution, even respected it. He just didn't find it very often in Clover.

"That's Peg, all right," he drawled, deliberately holding her gaze with his. "Taught my sister and half the females in Clover how to wait tables and bring home big tips without losin' their virtue."

"Believe me, Sheriff, I'm beyond the stage where I worry about my virtue." He watched the bitter curve of her lips and wondered about that, too. Before he could scare up more conversation, however, she was off.

Ford rubbed the back of his neck and gave some thought to the way she'd deflected his questions. Sophie didn't look like the kind of person who had anything to hide, but, still, he couldn't afford to give a newcomer too much slack. Even a small town cop learned right quick to expect the worst and act accordingly.

He dropped some money on the counter next to his still full cup of coffee, aware that he was tipping way too much. He figured a widow with a baby to support needed the money more than he did. Besides, it was the least a man could do for a woman he'd just decided to get into his bed, come hell or high water.

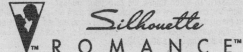

COMING NEXT MONTH

MILLION DOLLAR SWEEPSTAKES (III)

No purchase necessary. To enter, follow the directions published. Method of entry may vary. For eligibility, entries must be received no later than March 31, 1996. No liability is assumed for printing errors, lost, late or misdirected entries. Odds of winning are determined by the number of eligible entries distributed and received. Prizewinners will be determined no later than June 30, 1996.

Sweepstakes open to residents of the U.S. (except Puerto Rico), Canada, Europe and Taiwan who are 18 years of age or older. All applicable laws and regulations apply. Sweepstakes offer void wherever prohibited by law. Values of all prizes are in U.S. currency. This sweepstakes is presented by Torstar Corp., its subsidiaries and affiliates, in conjunction with book, merchandise and/or product offerings. For a copy of the Official Rules send a self-addressed, stamped envelope (WA residents need not affix return postage) to: MILLION DOLLAR SWEEPSTAKES (III) Rules, P.O. Box 4573, Blair, NE 68009, USA.

EXTRA BONUS PRIZE DRAWING

No purchase necessary. The Extra Bonus Prize will be awarded in a random drawing to be conducted no later than 5/30/96 from among all entries received. To qualify, entries must be received by 3/31/96 and comply with published directions. Drawing open to residents of the U.S. (except Puerto Rico), Canada, Europe and Taiwan who are 18 years of age or older. All applicable laws and regulations apply; offer void wherever prohibited by law. Odds of winning are dependent upon number of eligibile entries received. Prize is valued in U.S. currency. The offer is presented by Torstar Corp., its subsidiaries and affiliates in conjunction with book, merchandise and/or product offering. For a copy of the Official Rules governing this sweepstakes, send a self-addressed, stamped envelope (WA residents need not affix return postage) to: Extra Bonus Prize Drawing Rules, P.O. Box 4590, Blair, NE 68009, USA.

SWP-S795

He's Too Hot To Handle...but she can take a little heat.

SILHOUETTE

Summer Sizzlers

This summer don't be left in the cold, join Silhouette for the hottest Summer Sizzlers collection. The perfect summer read, on the beach or while vacationing, Summer Sizzlers features sexy heroes who are "Too Hot To Handle." This collection of three new stories is written by bestselling authors Mary Lynn Baxter, Ann Major and Laura Parker.

Available this July wherever Silhouette books are sold.

SOMETIMES BIG SURPRISES
COME IN SMALL PACKAGES!

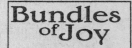

BABY TALK
Julianna Morris

Cassie Cavannaugh wanted a baby, without the complications of an affair. But somehow she couldn't forget sexy Jake O'Connor, or the idea that he could father her child. Jake was handsome, headstrong, unpredictable...and nothing but trouble. But every time she got close to Jake, playing it smart seemed a losing battle....

Coming in August 1995 from

Silhouette ROMANCE™

BOJ3

If you are looking for more titles by

ELIZABETH AUGUST

Don't miss this chance to order additional stories by
one of Silhouette's great authors:

Silhouette Romance™

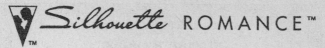

is proud to present

The spirit of the West—and the magic of romance! Saddle up and get ready to fall in love Western-style with the fourth installment of WRANGLERS & LACE. Available in August with:

Cowboy for Hire
by Dorsey Kelley

Benton Murray was a cowboy with secrets—and now the former rodeo hero only wanted to forget the past. Then spirited Kate Monahan came to him with big plans for her own championship. All she wanted was someone to rein in her natural talent. And soon Benton was finding it difficult to deny her the help she needed—or the passion he felt for her!

Wranglers & Lace: Hard to tame—impossible to resist—these cowboys meet their match.

As a *Privileged Woman,* you'll be entitled to all these *Free Benefits.* And *Free Gifts,* too.

To thank you for buying our books, we've designed an exclusive FREE program called *PAGES & PRIVILEGES™.* You can enroll with just one Proof of Purchase, and get the kind of luxuries that, until now, you could only read about.

*B*IG HOTEL DISCOUNTS

A privileged woman stays in the finest hotels. And so can you—at up to 60% off! Imagine standing in a hotel check-in line and watching as the guest in front of you pays $150 for the same room that's only costing you $60. Your *Pages & Privileges* discounts are good at Sheraton, Marriott, Best Western, Hyatt and thousands of other fine hotels all over the U.S., Canada and Europe.

*F*REE DISCOUNT TRAVEL SERVICE

A privileged woman is always jetting to romantic places. When <u>you</u> fly, just make one phone call for the lowest published airfare at time of booking—<u>or double the difference back!</u> PLUS—

you'll get a $25 voucher to use the first time you book a flight AND <u>5% cash back on every ticket you buy thereafter through the travel service!</u>

SR-PP3A

$\mathcal{F}$REE GIFTS!

A privileged woman is always getting wonderful gifts.
Luxuriate in rich fragrances that will stir your senses (and his). This gift-boxed assortment of fine perfumes includes three popular scents, each in a beautiful

designer bottle. <u>Truly Lace</u>...This luxurious fragrance unveils your sensuous side. <u>L'Effleur</u>...discover the romance of the Victorian era with this soft floral. <u>Muguet des bois</u>...a single note floral of singular beauty.

$\mathcal{F}$REE INSIDER TIPS LETTER

A privileged woman is always informed. And you'll be, too, with our free letter full of fascinating information and sneak previews of upcoming books.

$\mathcal{M}$ORE GREAT GIFTS & BENEFITS TO COME

A privileged woman always has a lot to look forward to. And so will you. You get all these wonderful FREE gifts and benefits now with only one purchase...and there are no additional purchases required. However, each additional retail purchase of Harlequin and Silhouette books brings you a step closer to even more great FREE benefits like half-price movie tickets... and even more FREE gifts.

L'Effleur...This basketful of romance lets you discover L'Effleur from head to toe, heart to home.

Truly Lace...
A basket spun with the sensuous luxuries of Truly Lace, including Dusting Powder in a reusable satin and lace covered box.

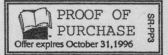

Complete the Enrollment Form in the front of this book and mail it with this Proof of Purchase.

PROOF OF PURCHASE
Offer expires October 31, 1996

SR-PP3